R^{7}/99 P^{v} Mystery
                       Dou
                       1999

The Cat and the King of Clubs

A Midnight Louie Las Vegas Adventure

Book 1

The Cat and the King of Clubs

A Midnight Louie Las Vegas Adventure

Book 1

CAROLE NELSON DOUGLAS

Five Star
Unity, Maine

Five Star Mystery.
Published in conjunction with Tekno Books and Ed Gorman.

June 1999
Standard Print Hardcover Edition.

Five Star Standard Print Mystery Series.

The text of this edition is unabridged.

Set in 11 pt. Plantin by Minnie B. Raven.

Printed in the United States on permanent paper.

Library of Congress Cataloging in Publication Data

Douglas, Carole Nelson.
    The cat and the king of clubs / by Carole Nelson Douglas.
        p.   cm. — (A Midnight Louie Las Vegas adventure ; bk. l)
    ISBN 0-7862-1920-3 (hc : alk. paper)
    I. Title.   II. Series: Douglas, Carole Nelson.   Midnight Louie
Las Vegas adventure ; bk. 1.
    [PS3554.O8237C24   1999]
    813′.54—dc21
                                                    99-24667

For Denise Little — a savvy publishing professional and first, last, and always a staunch believer in Louie and me; her indignation at the indignities the first Midnight Louie books suffered kept us going, and going, and going. . . .

♣ Author's Foreword ♣

It was January, 1990. I was mad as hell and not going to take it any more, but Midnight Louie was hissing, spitting, snarling furious.

I was just another good writer done wrong by an all-too-often indifferent or even punitive publishing world. But Midnight Louie, P.I. was a cat (and a dead one at that), who I had resurrected as a Sam Spade with hairballs. He was twenty pounds of politically incorrect alley cat, unfixed as yet, and not about to take being literarily neutered lying down.

The atrocity in question: five years after we had collaborated on an innovative and ambitious romance quartet with ongoing mystery elements, featuring ML as an intermittent, first person narrator, it was at last coming to print. But the editor had cut the four books up to 37 percent each without my knowledge or participation. (I call this "cutting the body to fit the coffin.")

I had entered publishing 13 years earlier during a time of rapid paper price increases and had been asked to cut my second novel by almost a half. But at least I was asked to cut it. The Midnight Louie quartet was axed unilaterally. I might never have found out before publication had I not asked where the galley proofs were.

Writers will often carry, branded on their souls, some gratuitously mean phrase an editor has used in rejecting their work. Every time I've heard Mary Higgins Clark speak, she quoted a magazine editor who found her early short fiction "light, slight, and trite."

The editorial phrase explaining the mistreatment of the Midnight Louie romance quartet is burned into my brain too: "too upmarket, mainstream, and sophisticated (for romance readers)."

But "upmarket, mainstream, and sophisticated" are not the cruelly dismissive "light, slight, and trite." They are good words. I was told my books were mistreated because they were too good!

The subsequent movement of many romance authors (Sandra Brown, Janet Evanovich, Tami Hoag, Nora Roberts) into mainstream bestsellerdom through an updated form of romantic suspense, interestingly enough, has given the lie to that short-sighted underestimation of the audience, and the writers.

During the five-year limbo in which the ML quartet languished (sold in early 1985, submitted in early 1986, published in mid-1990), the limited series became a romance fiction staple. Having my ground-breaking books languishing on the shelf made me wild with frustration. As an ex-newspaper reporter, I wanted the "scoop."

The Midnight Louie quartet was cutting edge, and I knew it, not the first "limited series" in the category romance field, but one of the first: *Love Boat* in Las Vegas.

I'd created an entire universe as a background, an updated Damon Runyon world that gave Louie his unique "voice," and used the contemporary wonderland of Las Vegas as a backdrop instead of the twenties and thirties Broadway that Runyon wrote about. I had an arsenal of continuing, colorful secondary characters, humor and suspense, an ongoing mystery that was solved in the fourth book.

But I had to watch, bound and gagged, while limited series and romantic suspense became hot new trends, and my ground-breaking series stayed on the shelf.

When the books finally were published, editor and house seemed determined to pull the quartet's teeth, concealing everything that was fresh and creative about them. The Las Vegas location and the black cat image were considered "too much mystery," so a proposed two-volume title of Las Vegas Days and Las Vegas Nights became Crystal Days and Crystal Nights. First Midnight Louie was going to be on the cover, then was taken off. (Nowadays readers complain that cats are put on covers of books they are barely in because publishers know they attract readers, who usually love cats.)

The romance buyer for a major bookstore chain told me later that she had "not been happy" with the books' covers and told the publisher so before publication — they didn't change a thing. They didn't care.

I knew they were wrong, wrong, wrong. Everything they feared about the books: Midnight Louie himself, the "upmarket, mainstream, and sophisticated" approach to love and larceny in Las Vegas, was a strength, not a weakness. So, out of frustration, betrayal, and feline fury, the Midnight Louie romance quartet (with ongoing mystery) evolved into the new Midnight Louie mystery series (with ongoing relationships).

There's a happy ending: I later encountered an editor who had seen the Midnight Louie quartet being shelved, but had now moved up the hierarchy. She felt so bad about what had happened that she helped me get the rights back. "It's the least we can do for this poor author," she told her superiors.

"This poor author," like many another caught in a publishing meat-grinder, had managed to hold on, go on, survive, and even thrive. Midnight Louie's mystery series now has eleven books in print (*Catnap, Pussyfoot, Cat on a Blue Monday, Cat in a Crimson Haze, Cat in a Diamond Dazzle,*

Cat with an Emerald Eye, Cat in a Flamingo Fedora, Cat in a Golden Garland, Cat in a Hyacinth Hunt, Cat in an Indigo Mood, and this fall's *Cat in a Jeweled Jumpsuit*.) Readers have embraced Louie in his new format, and have become curious about his earlier four books. I'm happy to finally satisfy that interest.

In preparing the first book of the ML quartet for publication, I restored material that had been cut, including forty percent of Louie's narrative sections. These were always briefer than they are in the current mystery series. Just having a cat narrator was daring enough in 1985–86; I made sure to keep his contributions short, if not sweet.

I've shortened the "sensual scenes." Mystery readers, and many romance readers today, don't need the detail that was demanded then.

Las Vegas has changed so much, so fast, and so radically since I researched and wrote this book in 1985 that I'm leaving the background "as was" to record what the city used to be like before fifteen years of spectacular boom. Because of the fast-forward nature of the Las Vegas scene, this is the pattern of the Midnight Louie mystery series too. The characters in the foreground glide through a time period of months while the background buildings whiz by, reflecting years of construction and de-construction. It's like early movies, where the actors play a scene in the unmoving car while a montage of background scenes fly by. That's the only sensible way to deal with The City That Won't Stop Reinventing Itself.

So here the quartet begins again, in a new, "authorized" edition. The credit goes, in the end, to readers, who live long, and don't forget. In that way, they're a lot like Midnight Louie, the alley cat who won't ever roll over and play dead.

♣ Chapter One ♣

Introducing Midnight Louie, P.I.

Las Vegas. It is Baghdad under glass. A neon bouquet to the whole wide world set in a doily of desert.

It is flash and flesh and glitter and cash. It holds enough busted bank accounts and broken hearts to pave the Interstate from Needles to the Big Sur. It is bag ladies and chorus girls . . . guys, dolls and Mafia dons . . . potentates and small potatoes . . . tipsters and tourists.

Vegas is people on the take, people on the make, people just out to have a good time — and win a little, maybe lose a lot.

It is my kind of town.

I was born here, weaned on a desert breeze and the sob of a showgirl's mother. I have been on my own since I could walk, and I have hoofed every overheated inch of this berg, every back alley and gaudy-awful overelectrified front street. I know every grain of sand from the Strip's neon fringes to where a guy can find a high-noon shady spot to snooze downtown. I do not sleep at night; not in Las Vegas, and miss the action.

They call me Midnight Louie.

It is in my veins, Vegas. There are times I might be wiser to skip town — I am no angel — but I stay and even try to go straight.

Now I am what you might call the unofficial house dick at the Crystal Phoenix Hotel and Casino . . . hell, all Las Vegas is one big overpopulated cosmic hotel open twenty-

11

four hours a day. Just like the wedding chapels.

So I know a lot of stories — sad, glad; sob, mob — you name it. I was outside the Sirocco Inn when Gino Scarletti bought it — not the inn, the farm, otherwise known as six feet of dirt, downward. But the cops never heard a peep from me. Midnight Louie is still light on his tootsies, even if he has acquired some pinch-worthy inches lately, and I rabbited that one.

I am also the silent type. It does not do to know too much in this town. Not that the tourists ever suspect half the stuff that goes on. Naw, to them Las Vegas is just "Lost Wages" or "Sin City," a three-day round-trip junket of blackjack, singing slot machines and free drinks with more paper umbrellas than booze in them.

Yeah, Las Vegas. It can be a mean town, but it has a heart as big as the sun when it sinks over the mountains like a red-hot five-dollar gold piece. I have never seen a hunk of neon to compare to a desert sunset. And I have never seen real lovers leave Las Vegas unhappy.

Nowadays, I do more thinking than anything. The years catch up, even to an old tomcat on the prowl like me. I do not say a lot these days, but I see everything. Like I say, I hang out mostly at the Crystal Phoenix, where I got an "in" with the management — okay, they owe me.

You could say if it had not been for Midnight Louie, the Phoenix would not be the classy, world-famous joint it is today. So I feel obligated to stick around and add some local color to the establishment, you know?

Anyway, the lowdown behind the Phoenix is a story I like to call "The Princess and the Prince" — well, let us lay it on the green felt, folks. Mr. Nicky Fontana is a prince of a guy, but the only blood that runs in his Family is red, not blue. And lots of it. Not that Mr. Nicky Fontana has ever had any time for that mob hanky-panky. Naw, he has been to college and is set on adding some legitimate luster to the Fontana es-cutch-eon. (See, I got *some* class.)

So there is this old hulk of an abandoned hotel right on the Strip, and there is Mr. Nicky Fontana with a few million in genuine clean dough inherited from his grandma's pasta factory in Venice — Venice, California, that is. Nicky is hotter than a Saturday night poker player to put his whole stash into turning the old Joshua Tree into the handsomest, classiest hostelry in Vegas — not the biggest, but the best.

Now Mr. Nicky's usual associates, they are not exactly hoity-toity. So he does what any guy with money and imagination usually does when he needs something he does not have . . . like class. He imports it.

I will never forget the day she blew in.

I am discreetly eyeballing the lobby of the Joshua Tree for salvage. I am not as young as I used to be and gotta take what I can. Besides, I did not have then the cushy job I have now, and the Joshua Tree was up for grabs.

Anyway, she comes in wearing pale summer linen from her shoulders to her shoes, wearing a hat, of all things, one of those wide straw jobs with a scarf built-in. Yup, a linen scarf. Saffron color, like the desert sand first thing in the morning when the sun is still cool.

So is she.

She just stands there dead center in the empty lobby, slowly peeling off some European-style sunglasses that are darker than the custom window tint on Boss Banana's stretch limo, and stares. I stare, too, but she does not notice me. Nobody ever does. That is why I am so good at my new job, if I do say so myself.

Her you notice. Wow. Eyes like Lake Mead on a sizzling

July day — Independence Day, maybe — deep dark blue eyes, so cool a guy wants to do the backstroke in them. I gotta admit, I am smitten. Some kitten.

But she is not impressed — not with Walter Maxwell, the top Vegas shyster who has escorted her in; not with what is left of the hotel; not with anything.

I figure it can only get worse, but she does not notice me. She notices every little thing around that scene but me. That is her first mistake. I know it will not be her last. Not with Mr. Nicky Fontana around. . . .

♣ Chapter Two ♣

"How long has the hotel been . . . like this, Mr. Maxwell?"

"You mean vacant? About six years. It's not brand new, but —"

"It's at least forty years old. Architecturally, that's ancient! When your law firm contacted me in Athens, I was led to believe this would be a redecorating project, not a full restoration."

"Redecoration, restoration — it amounts to the same thing. You do have a seven-and-a-quarter million dollar budget to work with, Miss von Rhine."

She turned to him, her blue eyes steelier than a midnight special. "Your letter said it was *eight* million. What happened to the missing seven hundred and fifty thousand?"

Walter Maxwell, a balding facile man in an open-necked shirt and summer-weight suit, shrugged. "It's, uh, been allocated for a special project."

"The *hotel* is a special project, and it was to be all mine. Why would I travel thousands of miles to this . . . oasis of kitsch . . . you call Las Vegas if I hadn't been lured by the chance to redo the hotel in style? Now, before I even get here, one-ninth of my budget is gone!"

"Ten percent."

"Is *everything* in this town a matter of percentage?"

"Please, Miss von Rhine. We're all risking a lot here. I know you left a prestigious position as assistant manager at the hotel in Athens, but you *will* be manager here, I promise you that. And — I can explain. Even better, I'll show you. This way, please. To the elevators."

She stepped gingerly over the lint-strewn, rumpled red carpeting, glancing down disparagingly from time to time, step to step. Even endless wear had not managed to mute the pattern's screaming, wall-to-wall baroque excess.

"New Italian industrial carpeting. Number one," she muttered, mincing over the litter.

Maxwell only nodded while he concentrated on spinning a massive metal ring to find the key to the private elevator, whose closed stainless steel doors stood at tight-lipped attention, framed by their exclusivity, slightly apart from the guest elevators.

Maxwell's chiming keys struck an eerie note in the deserted hotel lobby, echoing endlessly. Something dark skittered from behind a dead potted palm into the shadow cast by a chrome tube filled with more cigarette butts than sand.

The woman beside Maxwell seemed too indignant to sense the atmosphere, but he felt it. He'd been on edge ever since his limo had met her at McCarran Airport, a hop outside town.

She'd been cool and crisp even in the wilting Las Vegas 100-degree heat, eyeing his long, ice-blue Caddy as if it were a particularly dingy Tia Juana taxi. Privately, Maxwell doubted that Van von Rhine would unbend if the celestial trumpets sounded Judgment Day, something the more pious of Las Vegas' critics hopefully predicted daily for the city of perpetual pleasure.

He stroked thin greige strands of hair into place over his damp bald spot, fanning the straw boater he affected as he tailed her onto the elevator, and glanced her way.

Young, he told himself; she was too young to be so formidable; only twenty-four and too young to snag a commission as plum as this . . . except that her father had been the best hotel manager in Europe and she'd grown up in a string of world-class hostelries from Vienna to the Greek Isles.

Her blond eyebrows lifted briefly as the elevator light flicked through the floor numbers in succession and stopped on the last one — thirteen.

"That'll be the second thing changed," she murmured as she left the elevator ahead of him.

Maxwell breathed relief. If she was thinking of changing things, she wasn't fleeing back to Athens.

"What?" he asked blandly.

"The floor number. Traditionally, hotels skip the thirteenth floor — it's unlucky. I'm surprised to find it here in Las Vegas . . . after all, gamblers are born superstitious. We'll simply rechristen it 'fourteen.' "

"He might not like that."

" 'He?' "

"Let me . . . uh, this way." Maxwell flourished open a numberless door and ushered her through it the way Custer might have escorted the Seventh Cavalry to the Little Big Horn. "One of the, uh, penthouses."

"Penthouses? They are the least — the last — of my concerns, Mr. Maxwell. A hotel gets little return on a penthouse, unless as a status symbol to house certain insecure guests whose egos need boosting. I'd much rather see the kitchens." She began pinching off her beige knit gloves by the fingertips.

"Here in Vegas penthouses are really important for high rollers. And he . . . really should meet you."

" 'He?' You keep saying he, he, he. It sounds like you're giggling." She smiled to take the sting out of her comment.

Maxwell swallowed, thinking. She acted so damned British, so correct, so cool . . . just what the Boss had ordered. She would drive him nuts.

"Please, Miss von Rhine, sit down."

For once she did as he suggested without demur. But first she had to remove some fabric swatch rings, frowning as her eyes skimmed the patterns. She calmly studied the room. Maxwell did, too, suddenly seeing it through her ice-blue gaze.

They viewed a big, showy, empty room. Outdated foil-backed wallpaper made dizzy Op Art motions over every wall. A chrome circular staircase with a rococo rail snaked up the farthest wall, its risers choked with shag carpeting. Life-sized statues of imitation white marble in fake Greek-god style stood in uneasy nakedness, as if decorating a sleazy health club.

A round bar — bemirrored, bechromed and betrashed — was the living room's inflated focal point. Marbleized violet wallpaper in the semi-circular foyer behind them was water-stained — and benefitted from this accidental refinement of design. Odds and ends of hotel furniture sat at careless angles, every horizontal surface aswamp with wallpaper rolls, carpet sample books thrown down askew, and empty Styrofoam coffee cups.

"You did say the plans were for a quality hotel?" Van von Rhine inquired politely.

Maxwell was spared answering. Muffled sounds erupted from a closed door leading off the main room; then the door itself exploded open.

A man stood in the doorway, his white shirtsleeves rolled up to his elbows, expensive cream silk tie roughly pulled out of its double-Windsor knot, dark head twisted to pinch the phone receiver to his hitched shoulder. An unlit cigarette dangled magically from his full lower lip as he talked. Or cajoled.

"Nostradamus! Just quit trying to talk me out of it and

lay the bet. Indian Summer in the sixth. To win. No place, no show. To win. I got a feeling. Right, two-fifty."

He hung up, ran his fingers through curly near-black hair, then noticed his guests.

"Hey . . . great." He slammed down the phone, which seemed endowed with an interminably coiled cord, atop a pile of phone books that served as an informal end table. "Maxie, you've done terrific."

His animated face, tanned, lean, and alert, froze in outright evaluation as he studied the woman sitting in the opposite chair. She watched dark eyes sweep inching approval from her arched instep up her ivory-hosed leg, then over the lines of the stark linen sheath and her bare white arms to her face, which was growing haughtier by the second.

"Terrific." The man came close and perched easily on the broad arm of her chair, ignoring her automatic recoil. His square-fingered hand, impeccably manicured, tilted her chin toward the desert light streaming through windows along the west-facing wall.

"Class — even to the fillings in her teeth, Maxie. Platinum, I bet, hmm, baby?"

His overheated olive-black eyes seemed to strike her with all the finesse of scalding coffee, and she jerked angrily away.

The man spun to his feet, unnoticing. "You're thinking concierge, right, Maxie? I mean, she'd be wasted as the dining room hostess. And get one of those skinny-legged, ladylike French desks for the lobby." He glanced back and down. "So you can see *her* legs. Class is okay, but sex appeal's even better. Make sure the new manager knows about the desk. When is that bozo getting here anyway?"

She was standing now, indignation stiffening her into temporary silence. Maxwell leaped in where angels would have been hotfooting it in a hellishly opposite direction and attempted a proper, if simple, introduction.

"Nicky . . . This *is* the new manager."

The man wheeled to face the woman, then froze, arrested energy personified as she was now ice incarnate. "The von Rhine guy? Van von Rhine, you said. I'm not stupid —" She snorted delicately. "I remember names."

"*Miss* Van von Rhine," Maxwell repeated fatalistically.

They eyed each other: she and he; light and dark; ivory queen and ebony king across a cluttered board. The pawn was the only thing between them at the moment; Maxwell cleared his throat and kept silent.

"Miss . . . Van . . . von Rhine." Nicky was moving again, slowly, like a punch-drunk boxer who can see the fight card clearly at last. He ended up before her, extending his palm and a confident grin. "Sorry for the mix-up. Nicky Fontana."

She ignored his hand, drawing on her gloves, finger by dainty beige finger. Maxwell quailed. She turned to him, scenting rank panic and exploiting it.

"I believe your driver is waiting downstairs, Mr. Maxwell."

"Now, Miss von Rhine —" Maxwell moved between them, blocking her view of Nicky, who turned and strode to the window. "Don't let a misunderstanding upset you. The hotel needs you."

"I can see that. Desperately, to judge by these decorating samples."

"That's . . . uh, just for the thirteenth — er, fourteenth floor. This penthouse. Private. Nothing to do with the rest of the hotel."

"What a relief," she answered acidly. "And who is this man?"

Nicky wheeled to face her, his brown forearms crossed on his chest. " 'This' man is the bankroller. The man with the money, honey. I own the hotel."

"You!"

"Not publicly," Maxwell put in quickly. "Nicky is a sort of, well, think of him as a silent partner. All he'll do is live up here, uh, take a peek downstairs now and again, count the money. You know, kind of a —"

"Slum landlord?" she finished with impeccable diction.

Maxwell's already round shoulders slumped, and he slunk to a position outside the ring.

"Look." Nicky took a moment to scrape up an apologetic tone. "I'm, uh, sorry. What kind of a first name is 'Van,' anyway?"

"My name." Very clipped.

"Anyway . . . you're just what I wanted for the hotel. I don't even mind that you're a woman."

"All the better for 'class with sex appeal'?"

"Forget the sex appeal; I just failed my Nevada driver's-license eye test. Look, er, Miss von Rhine. A hotel is a business, you know that. You're selling something, even in those snooty European flophouses you manage.

"Here in Vegas, we sell flash, flesh, and fun. Only I want to do it first-class, see? Nothing obvious, but even class needs a little . . ." His right hand swayed back and forth all too expressively. "A little ooomph. Okay?"

"If you ache to hire 'oomph,' Mr. Fontana, I suggest you look in the chorus line at the Tropicana. That you can hire. You can't hire 'class'; you can't buy it; and *you* certainly can't recognize it!"

She threw a ring of samples on the phonebooks, which toppled in slow inevitability while they all watched, fascinated. "I'll say good day."

Nicky Fontana moved so fast, he was frozen into position by the door before she got there, one muscular forearm barring her way, the discarded sample ring dangling in his other hand like an ineffectual pendulum. But she paused.

"Okay," he conceded. "So I'm no connoisseur. Why do you think I had Maxie scour the world? And he found you. He says you're tops; you're what my hotel needs. I want to hire you. Just do what you do. I'll try to keep my mitts out of it. All I got is some money and a vision of what another really world-class hotel could do for Las Vegas. But I need . . ."

He glanced away, looking for words, his profile etched against a white column on the empty foyer walls as strikingly as a head on a Roman coin. His hand brandished the sample ring in frustration, then his fingers spread helplessly, his expression growing wryly appealing.

"I need you, Miss von Rhine," he said. "I need to hire somebody with class enough to tell me when to go jump in Lake Mead." Nicky smiled the smile that always wore down Nostradamus the bookie, various hard-hearted chorines, and even his godfather, Mario, who'd always wanted Nicky in the Family business.

A sapphire glint lit Van von Rhine's eyes for the first time.

"Now you tempt me, Mr. Fontana. I think I'd *like* to tell you to go jump in Lake Mead."

"I'm at your mercy." He looked as defenseless as a shark, all smooth, slippery facade and perfect white teeth.

She smiled coolly. "Not this afternoon. Mr. Maxwell promised to show me the rest of the hotel." Her gaze dismissed the gaudy penthouse suite. "The real part."

"Wait'll you see this done over. It's gonna be gorgeous." Nicky articulated the last word with passionate conviction. She looked away.

"I doubt it. But the rest of your hotel will be, Mr. Fontana. Or my name isn't Van von Rhine."

She swept out the faceless door, never turning her head to ensure that Maxwell trotted behind her. He did, of course, but first he cast an apologetic and beseeching glance at his boss, his pupils rolling like dice gone awry and coming up snake eyes.

Nicky remained in the doorway after the elevator doors had pinched shut on the pair and the yellow light above them had winked out. He pulled the unlit cigarette from his mouth and tossed it dartlike toward the ashtray cylinder in the hall. It landed dead center, in the sand.

What are little girls with class made of? Nicky mused. *Rosewater and bath powder, spun sugar and ivory, probably. The sweet, elusive scent of . . . lily of the valley.*

His youthful face softened, then his strong Roman nose wrinkled dismissively. *And icewater and vinegar,* he reminded himself.

Nicky Fontana slammed the door shut so hard the windows on the opposite wall rattled and the number on its face would have trembled, if there had been any.

♣ Chapter Three ♣

"Nicky's an impulsive guy, but he means well," Maxwell said uneasily.

"That's hardly an excuse — or a recommendation for a good working relationship."

Van von Rhine restlessly prowled the seventh-floor living room to which Maxwell had shown her. Once this had been part of a suite decorated in a garish ideal of elegance.

Now the once-loud drapes hung faded and frayed. A stale scent of industrial cleaner and cigarette smoke performed a genteel pas-de-deux in the shadowed air. In the distance, an air-conditioning unit strained and groaned like Atlas in its eternal battle to hold back the desert heat.

"We've, uh, just got this floor running — for staff — and the main floor where the kitchens are," Maxwell explained. "And the penthouse, of course."

"Of course."

Van lowered her large, floppy straw purse to the floor as if it bore lead ingots, reflecting that she'd been en route to this tawdry destination for twenty-four hours . . . and perhaps for as many years before that.

Untying her scarf, she drew the hat off as wearily as she had her gloves, revealing natural taffy-blonde hair coiled into a beige satin twist while Maxwell gawked. At the dusty windows, the sullen sunset was drawing a bloody shade on the bright, white-hot summer heat. Her figure made a still, detailed silhouette against the waning daylight.

"You should be pretty comfortable here," Maxwell said hopefully, privately doubting that Van von Rhine would find the Taj Mahal cushy enough for her taste.

"My accommodations are the least of it." She sighed and turned to face the room. "I really question whether I should stay at all."

Maxwell turned in his hat in his hands like an unwanted Frisbee. "Getting your job back at that luxury hotel in Athens seems unlikely," he ventured.

"Yes." Her voice was bleaker than her eyes had been in the lobby.

"And that was your first official hotel position. I imagine finding another would take some time, even with your late father's connections."

"Yes."

"But you'd do it," Maxwell said in a burst of wholly self-generated confidence. "Nicky, on the other hand —"

"Yes?"

"This is his only chance to make good, so to speak. The Family has been pressuring him to join the Fontana enterprises. They didn't send him to some California college to — going straight is his idea, and his grandma's cash is underwriting it. I guess I'm saying he needs you more than you need him."

"He needs something."

Van marched from the window, unerringly found the light switch, and flipped it. Incandescence flooded the room like a truth ray. The decor looked even shabbier, as Maxwell looked smaller and Van herself wearier.

"Do you mean to tell me," she asked Maxwell, "that a clan of hoodlums owns this hotel? That I've been hired by thugs?"

"No, no. Not them. Nicky. It's Nicky's joint. I mean, place. After a while, you get to talking like them. I've been the Fontana mouthpiece — er, family lawyer — for twenty years."

"You get to talking like them. Not I." Van shuddered delicately. "I can't imagine trying to get any work done with that Fontana person squatting atop the hotel like a . . . an undereducated jaguar! It's really quite impossible."

"Yeah, this old hotel would take a lot of work to get back on its feet again. Not much bark left on the old Joshua Tree."

"Not the hotel. Anything brick and mortar can be redeemed. And a Joshua Tree is a cactus and has no bark. I've done my research. When I said it was impossible, I was referring to Mr. Fontana. Do you believe for an instant that he'll really keep his ill-disciplined fingers out of anything, especially this hotel if it means that much to him?"

"No, but you need him."

Van glared.

"Yes, you do, Miss von Rhine. You don't know Vegas. Its history, its . . . uh . . . unique ambiance. Nicky does, down to his toenails. You can't bring the Joshua Tree up from the ashes unless you know what goes in this town — hotelwise."

Van winced at his grammatically gauche last word.

"Give it a chance," Maxwell pleaded. "Give Nicky a chance. If this doesn't go, that's it. He's back in the bosom of his Family and the hands of his uncle Mario, running numbers and learning the rackets, just like all his brothers."

"There are more like him?"

Maxwell nodded. "Almost a dozen. Rico, Aldo, Eduardo, Armando, Ernesto, Emilio, Julio, Giuseppe and Ralph. The Fontanas believe in keeping it in the Family, and there's a lot of Family to keep it in. Nicky's the youngest."

"He certainly can't be the most diplomatic . . . You're sure the financing for this venture is sound?"

"Triple-A untainted money. Dough of the first water. So help me." Maxwell pressed his pasty little palm to the lapel that covered the location of his heart.

Van, still skeptical, sighed again. "I'll stay for awhile then, and at least draw up a plan for the hotel's revitalization — if Mr. Fontana can be convinced to refrain from making a nuisance of himself."

"I'm sure he won't, no problem," promised Maxwell, backing out of the room with a series of placating salaams.

As his heel and posterior entered the ill-lit hall, an indignant yowl ricocheted off the corridor walls. Van rushed to the doorway, but saw only semidarkness arrowing away into absolute blackness.

"Not —" she began, thinking the worst, as any hotel manager might about a deserted building.

"Not rats," Maxwell reassured her. "Cats. They get in somehow, trying to escape the daytime heat or nighttime cold."

Van shivered and ran her hands down the bare white arms Nicky's espresso-colored eyes had warmed only a half hour before. "You make this climate sound like a hellish exercise in one extreme of discomfort or the other."

"Not at all, Miss von Rhine. You'll find Vegas as delightful as Majorca or Scorpios — and Nicky Fontana as tame as an iguana."

Maxwell was melting into the shadowed hall, an insincere Cheshire-cat grin on his face. Van turned back to the room and shut the door, automatically sliding the chain lock into place. All her life had been spent in hotels as busy as a Paris railway station, but this untended hulk struck her as spooky in its emptiness, in the way its abandonment imitated her own.

For thirty seconds she dueled an overwhelming impulse to pick up her hat, her purse, and her gloves, and flee the Joshua Tree as fast as her sleek Italian pumps could carry her. But she couldn't. She needed it, she thought sadly, this decrepit hotel with its impossible bankroller ensconced above in his pathetically déclassé lair. She needed a job history longer than three months at the Athens hotel because Nikos Skaliedes had felt sorry for her after her father's death.

Van von Rhine had absolutely no credentials for a hotel career, other than twenty-four years of spending every waking and sleeping moment in a chain of hostelries from Bruges in the north of Western Europe to Athens on the selvage edge of Eastern Europe as her father had managed his way across continent.

Perhaps the unsettled life had contributed to her mother's early death. Certainly Althea von Rhine was only a name on an American birth certificate — Van had come into this world at the Sheraton Russell in New York City.

Now Erik von Rhine, too, seemed as remote as her unremembered mother. He had been an almost godlike figure to his only daughter; his death last year at the Venice Ritz had enshrined him permanently at a respectable distance.

There were a lot of things Van needed, she knew — a job, some time to think, to do something on her own, and not just because she was her father's daughter. The last thing she needed in this brave and battered new world she faced was a silent partner named Nicky.

"Give the kid a break, Nicky. She's fresh out of the eggshell."

"She's fresh out of the deep freeze. That chick could make a glacier look cozy."

"You're not hiring a chorus girl, Nicky. She's a pro. Her dad ran the best hotels in Europe. You said you wanted class."

"Class, not . . . not a Nazi in pantyhose!"

Nicky slung aside an armful of fabric swatch rings and
sank onto the sorely tried penthouse armchair. He pulled a
cigarette from a mother-of-pearl case and balanced it in his
fine-tipped fingers, contemplating it as solemnly as Hamlet
musing on the skull of Yorick.

"The old man was a German aristocrat, but her mother
was American," Maxwell pointed out. "Say, are you going to
light that cigarette with your burning glance alone or go
ahead and smoke the damn thing?"

Nicky looked up, a smile pulling his lips from a brooding
to a sunny expression.

"Hey, Maxie, you're not letting our semiaristocratic lady
get on your nerves, an ace mouthpiece like you?" He stuck
the cigarette jauntily in the corner of his mouth, unlit. "I'm
quitting smoking. Uncle Mario said this is how to do it.
When I'm off the nicotine, I throw away the habit of having
a cigarette in my hand." He glowered again. "That's just
what I need when I'm quitting smoking, an uptight dame
around."

Nicky stood, tossed his virgin cigarette into an ashtray
overflowing with crushed but unsmoked cylinders, and
thrust his hands into his pockets.

"I bet under that hat she even wears her hair in one of
those skinny, tight little rolls up the back of her head, like a
schoolteacher."

"It's called a French twist, and is considered elegant,"
Maxwell said prissily.

"Where? In the French Foreign Legion?"

"In society circles."

"Maybe this is a mistake. Maybe the dame is right; you
can't buy class. Maybe me and Vegas don't need it. We've
both done okay without it for a long time."

Maxwell peered closely. Nicky seemed to be laughing slyly at himself. All the Fontanas were volatile, by temperament and by the nature of their lives on just the wrong side of the law.

Nicky, being youngest, had been spoiled and ignored, loved and underestimated until two sides of his personality warred with each other — the desire to be part of them, and the loner urge of his youth. He had more potential than any of the Fontana boys, more hope, more heart. It must have made him feel guilty.

"Look, Nicky. Your grandma had a lot of faith in you. Eight mill was mucho dough to leave to a twenty-six-year-old guy, and only a grandson. Your uncle Mario's still steaming about it."

"Yeah. I sometimes wonder if he's more anxious to have me — or Mama Tinucci's money — in the business." Nicky brought a fresh cigarette consideringly to his lips. "Van von Rhine. It sounds like the name of a German railroad: the Van von Rhine Line."

"Get off that shtick with the girl! Think of her as a business associate, like me." Nicky made a derisive sound. "She can help you get what you want more than anything in this world, Nicky, more than a big win at the track, or some red-headed hoofer in the 'Lido' chorus line.

"She can help you put this no-name dump on the map, the Las Vegas map, right up there with the MGM Grand and Caesars Palace. Think of it. Your name in neon: Fontana Hotel." Maxwell's small hands spread wide as they limned the imaginary logo on air.

Nicky sat up, the cigarette rolling out of his mouth into his waiting palm as he lit up without benefit of matches.

"My name? You think so, Maxie? I hadn't considered re-naming the hotel yet. The Fontana Hotel." His mobile mouth kissed the air contemplatively. "Yeah, the 'Fontana.' I like that. It's got class."

"Sure. The Dunes, the Sahara, the Fontana. It's as natural as nachos. But first . . ." Maxwell perched on the chair arm, his straw hat hooked on his dapper knee. Nicky leaned close as the lawyer's voice lowered. "First you gotta research the thing. Get together with your new expert. Pick her brain."

"Brain. Now that I grant you. That doll has definitely got a first-class brain."

"Right. So all you have to do is take her out, show her the competition, and draw up a battle plan to make the Fontana the hottest hotel this old town ever set its bleary old eyes on."

"Right," Nicky said automatically. Then he frowned. "What do you mean, 'take her out'?"

"Show her the town, the hotels, the Strip."

"At night, like? Just her and me? Together?"

"Night would be a good start. Impress her with the Strip at full power, so she sees what a hotel is up against in this town."

The cigarette in Nicky's palm suffered from a sudden fatal crushing.

"Maxie, you want me to be seen — in public, all up and down the Strip — with this, this von Rhine chick? This ice-cube dame?"

"I think the term you're searching for is 'lady,' " Maxwell put in dryly.

"Yeah. With this out-of-it lady? No way. Work with her, okay. For the sake of the Fontana. But take her around? Someone might think I'd asked her out, or something. What about my reputation?"

"I thought you planned on being the White Sheep of the Family?"

"Business is one thing. But —"

"No more buts, Nicky. If you're serious about remaking this hotel, you'll get on that phone, dial room seven-eleven and ask Miss von Rhine out to dinner as pretty as you please. Prettier, in fact. Remember, you're not talking to Nostradamus the bookie or that Roxelle tootsie at the Tropicana. This is a lady, so you gotta play the little gentleman."

Nicky finally took the phone Maxwell extended like some instrument of torture and dialed the sparse, in-house numbers. He held it on his shoulder, while waiting — not hoping — for an answer.

"Maybe uncle Mario is right," he muttered, his knuckles whitening on the receiver. "The hotel game is no business for a Fontana."

♣ Chapter Four ♣

Nicky dubiously eyed his own reflection, an image of sartorial perfection — or what passed for it in a flashy town like Vegas: open-necked ivory silk shirt, wool-and-silk blend Italian suit the color of cappuccino, creamy Sicilian lambskin loafers.

The deserted, dimly lit hotel hallway lent a *Casablanca* air of tropical decline to Nicky's normally buoyant figure. He looked like a man bound for his own funeral, or at least for an appointment with his uncle Mario's most dedicated competitors.

Something rustled down the lengths of shadow stretching between each feebly beaming wall sconce; Nicky almost jumped out of his elegantly tailored Italian clothes. Sweet fettuccine! He hadn't felt this nervous since he'd asked Angel O'Malley, the Orange County High Pompon Queen, to the prom.

He frowned threateningly at his own craven image in the hallway mirror, turned and knocked briskly on the door to room 711, right below the tarnished brass numbers.

It opened instantly, almost as if she, too, had been pausing behind the door, nerving herself to face the inevitable — him.

Nicky cleared his throat, a hesitancy his associates would have regarded as foreign to the Nicky that they knew and loved. But then the Nicky that everyone knew and loved wouldn't have stood for being suckered into squiring the uptightest dame since Carrie Nation around Las Vegas, either, he reflected bitterly.

"Seven-come-eleven," Nicky noted insouciantly by way

of greeting, glancing to the numbers.

"I beg your pardon?" Eyebrows pale as corn silk elevated in scrupulously polite mystification.

"Your room number is a card-playing phrase. I don't know if it's lucky or unlucky. How's your room, anyway? Maxie's been trying to keep at least some part of the hotel liveable until it's redone."

She ebbed aside to admit him while Nicky scanned the shabby, once-grandiose decor. He shrugged.

"I've seen worse." Her earlier reaction to his own quarters rose vividly to mind. He grinned, looking more like the happy-go-lucky, devilishly winning Nicky his legions of friends, fans, and hangers-on would recognize. "So have you, I guess."

"Yes, but the condition of my room is immaterial. It's what . . . we . . . do with the other four hundred and thirty-nine rooms that matters."

"Exactly right," Nicky couldn't help approving. "There are four hundred and forty guest rooms in the old Joshua Tree. It's not the biggest hotel in town, but it's no doll house, either."

"That's a good size for a hotel," Van conceded. "Most European hotels are smaller; we're not used to gargantuas with three thousand rooms, like your MGM Grand and Caesars Palace."

"That's nothing," Nicky rejoined quickly. "The new Goliath has four thousand rooms. And the Sultan copped a smart shtick; it's got one thousand and one rooms — you know, like the *Arabian Nights* stories. Tough luck that we can't do something catchy with four hundred and forty rooms. But maybe class is better," Nicky conceded sagely.

Van von Rhine's face paled, if that was possible. She glanced down at herself with a self-dismissing fillip of her lips. "I hope I've dressed properly for . . . for what Mr. Maxwell calls 'Las Vegas's unique ambiance.' "

That tore it. Nicky was forced to do what he'd been fervently avoiding; he had to look at her. Now that she'd invited his inspection, he took his time.

She wore a cocktail dress, which was okay because some dames liked to dress to the incisors when out on the town in Las Vegas. The same silken cobalt hue that wrapped itself sleekly around her body polished her high-heeled sandals.

The outfit had a wide ruffle at the waist that Nicky had heard called a peplum, and its long tight sleeves and bodice were made of some net stuff that looked hot despite its transparency. The bodice itself was strapless, although on her the gown seemed as proper as if it had been on Sister Mary Ignatius from Holy Redeemer grade school. So maybe the dress was cool enough for a Las Vegas steambath of a night, Nicky thought; certainly she couldn't have had much on underneath — not that showed anyway. . . .

Nicky reached into his breast pocket for his mother-of-pearl cigarette case and clutched it pacifyingly.

"Looks okay," he said. "Might be a little warm, though, for the weather."

Her face fell under the sleek taffy hair pulled into his least favorite hairstyle; an updo of any nationality, even French, translated to "old maid" in Nicky's book.

"It's the most lightweight thing I brought," von Rhine was fussing, as if maybe Las Vegas was getting to that unshakable cool of hers. "Just how hot can it get here?"

"Hot as Hades," Nicky said authoritatively, opening the door for her exit. "Hot as . . . hell, to put it in the local lingo."

She sashayed out ahead of him, the peplin waggling perkily. Nicky was in no mood to notice. His cigarette case, carrying a full complement of unfiltered foreign cigarettes as untasted as the night so far, remained a reassuringly ready weight in his almost weightless suit coat.

Nicky nostalgically fingered the gold lighter in his pants pocket, like a Buddhist his prayer beads. If he didn't fall off the wagon and light up tonight, it'd be a miracle.

They stood together at the intersection of Flamingo and Las Vegas Boulevard, a street better known the world over as The Strip. The traffic light took its own sweet time doing anything, like a tapped player with only so many more chips to risk. Then it flashed them a green circle of "go" and they crossed.

Nicky had Van von Rhine by her elbow, a stiff impersonal projection he considered about as sexy as a pump handle. Around them, Las Vegas's eternally changing kaleidoscope of pedestrians — bermuda-short-clad tourists mingling with dark-suited businessmen and gold-lamé-swathed ladies of the perpetual Las Vegas evening — pressed together like a catch of thronging kippers.

"I hear this is now the busiest intersection in the world," Nicky explained with tour-guide pride. "It's outjammed even Times Square."

"They have a lot in common," Van commented acidly when she teetered on the opposite curb at last.

Nicky led her from the intersection, where somebody might career into them, and steered her into the icy blast emanating from the open doors of the over-airconditioned Barbary Coast casino. All the casinos were dark, chandelier-lit deep freezes in savvy contrast to the hot, neon-illuminated night outside. The jingle of slot machines chimed a seductive message all the way to the curb, catching the ears of passing gamblers.

Van von Rhine had masked her face with a dazed expression ever since Nicky had pulled his custom-silver Corvette into the valet parking line in front of the MGM Grand. He'd started with the Grand because it was the most dignified hostelry in Las Vegas — how was he to know the bronze maidens riding the dolphins in the front fountain were also blatantly clutching their own . . . bosoms?

When he was with Van von Rhine, Nicky noted sourly, he found himself censoring even his internal vocabulary. Those statues were sensuous ladies, all right, he had thought, bustling her past them. Funny he'd never noticed that before. But she had. There wasn't much Van von Rhine didn't notice, which might be good for the Fontana, professionally speaking, but personally, for him, it was a pain in the neck.

"That's the Dune's newest casino, that round black glass building with the neon palms," Nicky said, figuring it was time to point out local landmarks. "Down the block is the Hilton Flamingo and the Imperial Palace. Speaking of palaces, Caesars (no apostrophe) is right across from us — see that big statue of the draped dude on the horse? I think that's Caesar. Or one of 'em. There were a whole bunch of Caesars. Must have been a big Italian family. . . ." No chuckle from von Rhine, not even a smile. "So. You're the boss. What do you want to see first?"

She shivered, whether from a chill wind of escaping air-conditioning or some icy qualm more internal it was hard to say.

"You're the guide, Mr. Fontana. I'm at your mercy." She said it like she meant it.

"Everybody calls me Nicky," he responded, annoyed.

Her eyes darted to his face, their color as electric as the bright blue neon edging the Imperial Palace's pagoda roof lines. "I'm not everybody, Mr. Fontana."

"No . . . I see what you mean." He dropped her elbow like a hot potato. Let some baize-blind craps player plow right into her; he wasn't a nursemaid. "We'll try Caesars first; it's pretty spectacular," he added hopefully.

They passed the giant statue of a mounted Caesar on the corner without incident, and once on the escalator ramp floating tourists over stretches of hard concrete sidewalk, Nicky relaxed.

Ahead of them the colossal white erection that was Caesars Palace unrolled its magnificence. A long entry driveway featured a central chain of lighted fountains spearheaded by a reproduction of headless Winged Victory. The semicircular facade of columns fronting the hotel proper sheltered looming marble goddesses of antiquity, each the replica of some world-renowned statue.

"Venus." Nicky paused reverently at the foot of one white giantess.

"I know the piece," Van von Rhine said in tones quarried from pure Carrarra stone. "I've seen the original." She turned on him, a stiletto of midnight-blue arctic sky, and stabbed. "The whole point of classical statuary, Mr. Fontana, is its rarity; its uniqueness. You can't simply copy them wholesale and line them up" — her hand gestured eloquently to the line of semidraped and undraped female figures — "like, like hookers waiting for a pickup. It's hopeless, trying to make you understand! It's simply not a . . . very . . . classy . . . thing . . . to do."

Nicky swallowed. Behind the marble ladies, he saw a smattering of all-too-fleshy life-size women plying their trade. Hookers were almost as ubiquitous a Las Vegas commodity as casino chips.

Cars swept up the curved approach to Caesars Palace — Mercedes, Cadillacs, and costly custom jobs wearing more

38

chrome than paint. The spotlit, dancing sprays of water, the gleaming fenders and chrome seemed to tarnish under the cold blue glare flashing from the eyes of an angry goddess in azure silk.

"I'm just showing you what's considered classy in Vegas," Nicky extemporized. "I didn't say I thought it was. Anyway, we're eating at the Dune's Dome of the Sea restaurant tonight and catching the late show at the MGM Grand."

But first they toured the interior of Caesars Palace, a string of vast, marble-pillared casinos and cocktail lounges. They strolled along its echoing Appian Way of expensive shops, including Cartier, Gucci, and others even more pricey until they came to another sculpted reproduction — Michelangelo's *David*, a towering tribute to the naked male form, placed so that it could only be viewed at a sharp upward angle.

"I suppose you've seen this guy before too," Nicky said glumly.

"I've seen the original 'copy' in a square in Florence near the Pitti Palace where the real original is displayed for its protection," she agreed.

"Tacky, too, huh?" He stared up wistfully at David's yeasty thighs.

"Well, look! You can't see anything of the statue at such a foreshortened distance. A heroic sculpture has to be placed where it can be viewed in a larger architectural context. Here, everybody gets to look up David's kilt, which he doesn't happen to be wearing."

"Right." Nicky hastily backed away from the statue before he was forced to confront the obvious too closely. Until he'd escorted Van von Rhine, he hadn't realized the old town was so raunchy.

At last they emigrated down the street to the Dune's geodesic restaurant, plunging into its deliberate aquatic dimness. They were seated immediately in a banquette where they could momentarily elude each other behind the long, glossy menus offering hors d'oeuvres priced in the double-digits.

Van von Rhine glanced up from her menu long enough to study the ranks of crystal-hung chandeliers suspended over the intent gambling heads in the casino beyond them like so many diamond-teethed circular saws about to descend.

"Apparently Las Vegas has a crystal fetish," she observed. "I haven't seen so much cut glass since the busboy at the Athens hotel tripped and brought down the entire water-goblet-supply table."

"Yeah," Nicky admitted. "That's what Las Vegas is for — lights. And glitter. And having fun." Nicky, who wasn't having any fun at all, had enunciated the last phrase darkly. "What are you going to order?"

She sighed. "Overpriced, all of it. The fish of the day, I suppose."

"Oh?" He studied his menu with mock care. "Carp?"

"Not classy, Mr. Fontana," her low voice purred.

Nicky glanced up to see that his jibe had sparked the crystal glitter now refracting from her eyes. It'd burn her up to know their vivid color reminded him of the glitzy blue sparkle of spotlighted rhinestones.

"Look," he said disarmingly. "Nobody calls me Mr. Fontana. That's my uncle when he's in a bad mood and everybody's walking on glass. If we're gonna be working together —"

She lowered the menu to regard him. "I don't suppose anybody ever called you Nicholas."

This time *he* winced. "Not since Miss Pribble in third grade, and she got glue in her drawer."

"Heavens! I'd hate to think what you'd do to retaliate now that you're all grown up. Well, how about Nick, then? Close enough?"

He shrugged. "Close enough, I guess. I'm used to being Nicky, though; why not, I'm the youngest."

"You're not in your family now . . . Nick." Mr. Fontana obviously had been a tonguetip away. "If you're going to be a major hotelier, you'll need a more dignified form of address, even among . . . intimates."

She articulated the last word like it was poison, he noticed before answering. "All I can say is, it was good enough for Nicky Hilton."

"You should do so well." But she smiled.

Maybe the trick was getting Van von Rhine off her feet and off the streets, Nicky thought. Out of the heat. Maybe now that he had a chance to lavish the Fontana charm on her, he could warm up the relationship. Maybe she was just melted caramel inside, after all. Maybe green pigs could whistle Dixie and Nostradamus could be found when it was his turn to pay up. . . .

Nicky — aka Nick now — smiled gamely back. "Order what you like," he advised her. "It's on the house. My house."

"A house is not a hotel, Mr. — Nick. And what you have sitting on ten acres of prime Las Vegas Strip is only an idea waiting to happen at the moment. It's going to take a lot of planning, money, hard work and time to accomplish. If it's worth it," she added under her breath just as the waiter came for their order, so Nicky couldn't answer her.

"Reopening the Joshua Tree is a great opportunity, you know," Nicky said, suddenly serious. "Most Vegas hotels are owned by big corporations now — not much room for the personal touch. And not everybody can get the Nevada Gaming Board to okay a new operation. Look at the Jockey Club down the Strip, a brand-new building that never opened. Everything around it is languishing. See, things either go big in this town, or they don't go at all."

She looked at him for a long moment without answering, until he started feeling as if he should fidget — as if he were Nicky Fontana, all right, back in fourth grade, and he'd been caught playing with a pocketful of dreams in geography class.

He'd stood up to his nine older brothers; he'd defied his uncle Mario, which nobody who wasn't Family — and some who were — did without paying for it; he'd staunchly resisted the pleas of his widowed mother.

All for what Nicky wanted to do more than anything in his glittery world, including chasing dice or women or newer and flashier cars. He wanted to make a first-class hotel out of an abandoned hulk of empty rooms and run-down dreams on the Las Vegas Strip.

Now, with nothing between him and Van von Rhine's clear, assessing eyes but his heart and soul, for the first time Nicky Fontana wondered if he could really do it.

But dinner was better, almost amiable. She ordered the most expensive entrée, lobster Pernod, having taken Nicky at his word that the meal was on him. Around them and the other diners, tropical fish glided through the illuminated azure waters of their gigantic tanks while the dining room harpist plucked liquid melodies from delicate strings.

"I guess you didn't get much to eat on the plane," Nicky suddenly realized as their dinner plates were cleared. "It was a long trip here."

"Yes." She sipped the anisette that accompanied her coffee as if thinking of something else — as if she *were* somewhere else . . . or wanted to be.

Nicky got up to leave the banquette and extended a helping hand. "Ready? The late show at the MGM's starting in half an hour."

She seemed to read his angry uncertainty etched in the lines of Nicky's outstretched palm. Finally, she put one graceful hand into his custody and let him lever her up and out into the hot, frenetic Las Vegas night. Dames, Nicky thought fiercely. So weak and yet so strong. . . .

Although they'd never left the quintet of hotels clustered around the intersection, three-and-a-half hours had passed and the number of passersby had tripled.

They stood, together again, at the interminable red light, heat heavy as molten lead pressing down upon them from the opaque black sky beyond the pulsing canopy of lights.

Nicky noticed nothing but the general glitter, the wired, go-for-it nervous energy boiling all around him.

Then he noticed that Van was gazing at a single sequin of half-lit moon hung in the night-jet sky — all of the heavenly fireworks that the winking neon around them would let them perceive: just that blue-white, luminous intensity making the half-moon a unwitting twin to every lozenge of mercury vapor street lining the Strip.

Down the street the Flamingo's show sign neurotically twitched its pink neon fan of tailfeathers and the Barbary Coast's carnival of red and yellow lights spun like a carousel. Behind them orange-and-green neon palms swayed electrically against the black-glass Deco donut of the Dune's casino. All around them came and went men in track suits and women in shorts, bottle-blonds and balding businessmen.

Van clutched her purse, starting at the brush of the unfamiliar fabric of Nick's jacket. He seemed as overdrawn as the entire scene, his lush dark Italian looks as high-calorie as the hot-fudge sundae of undiluted glitz melting in the late-night heat all around them.

He was crazy; they all were, Van thought desperately. Las Vegas meant "the meadows" in Spanish; the guidebook she had bought at McCarran Airport revealed that on page one. Yet nothing but barren sand remained here now; sand and the absurd artificial playground that had been erected atop it. Oh, Nicky Fontana might be serious enough, sincere enough about his desire to make something of the old Joshua Tree Hotel, out of himself.

But he needed her to do it, she told herself with some satisfaction. Mr. Maxwell had been right about that. And Van von Rhine did not believe in making sandcastles. Not any more. Not after Munich.

The light changed. Van was swept along with the crowd champing at its single electronic bit to migrate from the Dunes to the MGM to the Barbary Coast to Caesars Palace to the Flamingo Hilton in an endless, four-square round.

"Oh," said Van, dragging Nicky to a stop just inside the icy MGM-Grand lobby as she viewed the immense vista of royal red carpeting and crystal-strung crowns of chandeliers sandwiching the hotel's dark main-floor casino between them like roast beef on rye.

Nicky propelled Van past lines of people to the theater entrance where swagged velvet ropes separated the mob from the VIPs. A long pink card in Nicky's hand wafted them past the guard to a black-tie attired maitre d' who ushered them into a red-velvet plush banquette inside.

Van stared at the opulent house, at its semicircular tiers of tables and the stage as vast as the Milan Opera House's.

"Fourteen hundred seats," Nicky said. "One of the biggest houses in Vegas. We won't have anything this size, of course. I figure a nice intimate revue. Not too nude. Classy. But you should see how the big shows are done."

Van said nothing, not even when the waiter came and, after taking Nicky's order, returned with an ice bucket, three shot glasses apiece, and a pair of lowball glasses crammed with ice cubes as big as huge, uncut diamonds.

"Gin keeps best over the show," Nicky explained as he bartered a ten dollar tip for the drinks, which were included in the ticket price and therefore, in the parlance of commercial establishments everywhere, "free."

"I . . . uh . . . feel like John Wayne." Van eyed her winking lineup of shot glasses.

"Nurse 'em," Nicky advised. "This is a long show and everybody gets here early. This stage set-up" — he waved at the closed curtains of the proscenium arch towering not fifty feet away — "is second only to the Metropolitan Opera House in New York City. They've got eleven elevators for sets and stuff. It's really something."

Van took a swallow of gin, which helped her hold her tongue. She wasn't going to argue with him, but he had to show her first.

Nicky just sat back, as if he had never had anything to prove, which only made Van suspicious. Finally the gilt-fringed curtain rolled back its massive velvet folds. All the lights, action, and glitter of Las Vegas pooled into a treasure hoard of onstage motion and music.

Van sipped her way through the shot glasses in the dark, watching chorus girls strut across the stage wearing rhinestone bikinis and enough feathers to furnish an ostrich herd. Acrobatic male dancers were even more scantily clad.

The first act ended with a literal roar when "Leo," the MGM-lion — in the flesh and regal ruff of fur — burst through a paper hoop to rumble impressively at the audience.

Something tickled Van's ear and she jumped.

It was only the faint vibration of Nicky's nearby whispering lips.

" 'Jubilee' cost ten million bucks to mount. It's been running for almost four years and has another six to go. Pretty hot stuff, huh?"

While a set of muscular Balkan acrobats jumped to incredible heights atop each other's shoulders in front of the closed curtain between acts, Van glanced to Nicky.

"How do you know so many statistics?" she asked.

He shrugged modestly while scanning the menu-sized program illustrated inside with photos of two gorgeous chorines who obviously believed that sequins — and darn few of them — were a girl's best friend.

"I . . . uh, used to know somebody in the cast."

"Some body . . ." Van echoed knowingly, mentally separating the single word into its two, more accurately descriptive components.

"Listen to this," she frowned at the program's back credits. 'Company Manager . . . FLUFF LECOQUE.' Who'd believe a name like that was real?"

"I happen to know it is." Nicky's hand pressed his pale wool lapel to his heart. "That's her honest, birth-certificate moniker, so help me. I know the lady."

Van still looked skeptical.

"Besides, who'd believe a name like 'Van von Rhine' anyway?" he added impishly.

She frowned and snapped her program shut just as the stage curtain swirled apart again.

Act II revealed a set as elaborate as one in any production of *Aida*. While a narrator outlined the familiar story, chorus and lead performers danced the tale of Samson and Delilah. It climaxed, following an erotic pas de deux between the title couple, when the chained Biblical strong man pulled down the pillars of the Philistine temple and forty feet of artful set tumbled interminably against a hellish backdrop of flashing red flames.

Nicky Fontana leaned so close Van felt his breath insinuate itself under the sheer neckline of her dress. His arm stretched casually along the banquette behind her, so there was no escape in pulling back.

"I bet," he said speculatively, "I bet you find all of this somewhat —"

"Yes?" Let *him* put the obvious into words for a change, Van thought righteously.

"Well, the leather-clad chorus boys, the dancing girls, the topless Samson — not to mention . . ." His eyes flicked stageward. "Not to mention Delilah. I'd bet a bundle that you find the whole sordid little story and its reenactment pretty . . ." Van could hardly wait for him to finish it.

"Philistine," he hissed silkily into her ear.

She jerked around to face him. He was laughing at her.

"Vulgar was the word I had in mind," she snapped.

"It's good clean, dirty fun," he answered. "Just think of it as a Cecil B. DeMille movie."

"Must I?" Van turned back to the stage and watched while a between-act magician made a sequin-draped female assistant vanish and reappear in a series of clever illusions. Van almost wished she could trade places with the woman in the mask of stage makeup and sink through the invisible stage trapdoor into obscurity.

But the audience around her was rapt, as she found herself becoming, too. No matter how elongated the chorus girls' false eyelashes or how abbreviated their glittery

47

G-strings, she had to concede that they were splendid athletes able to move effortlessly despite the burden of forty-pound headdresses.

By the final act, when lights changed with dizzying regularity and the ensemble pranced in ever more spectacular costumes down a towering flight of onstage stairs while the chorus sang and danced with movie-musical fervor, Van felt like a child transported to the far end of an endless kaleidoscope of dazzling, flickering fantasy images.

The curtain closed to thunderous applause and ovation after ovation.

Finally benumbed from clapping, Van found her palm curled around her empty glass, the ice cubes entirely melted and the shot glasses empty. A slightly scratchy sensation impinged on her shoulders. Van discovered that she was leaning unconsciously into Nicky's arm behind her.

She sat bolt upright. "Well."

"Yes?" Nicky had mellowed after a couple enforced hours in a passive spectator's seat. "I bet you hated it," he observed complacently.

"How *much* would you bet?" Van's eyes narrowed.

Her challenge surprised him, but he pursed his lips consideringly. "A day at your command."

Her eyes outglittered stage-lit rhinestones. "Tempting. But I'm afraid I'm a convert. It was really rather impressive, once one accepted the . . . ambiance."

He shrugged uneasily. "I lose, then."

"Yes, you do, because you're going to owe me several days at my command. I can see I need to study Las Vegas from top to bottom before I can begin to comprehend what your hotel needs in the way of theme, decor and presentation. You're going to introduce me to the finer points of everything in Las Vegas from buffet lunches to shows in the buff. And we won't stop until I'm suitably impressed."

"What made you change your mind?" he asked.

"Because if I hadn't it might have given you some satis-faction to see me turn tail and run," she answered, rising from her seat. She paused before entering the crowded aisle. "And I don't wish ever to be accused of giving you satisfac-tion."

The crowd was pressing into the aisles and funneling its slow way out. Nicky escorted Van into the trickling exit line and mulled over her words.

He had been Vegas-wise enough to get VIP tickets for easy entree; he couldn't do a damn thing to hurry their way out. And that's how it was going to be with the hotel and Van von Rhine, he thought, watching her sleek, non-commital figure inch forward ahead of him.

Getting yourself into something is a snap, isn't it, Nicky, boy? he asked himself. Uncle Mario was right. Getting out will be too damn much like work.

♣ Chapter Five ♣

MIDNIGHT LOUIE INJECTS A WORD

One thing about Vegas is crystal clear: Word gets around very quick in this town.

So it is not long before insiders all up and down the Strip are chattering like a pair of hot dice over Mr. Nicky Fontana and his "new lady."

One rumor has it she is an English countess whose husband took the top-floor dive from his hotel due to some unwise investments at the baccarat table. Another story speculates that she is a German geologist who has found silver under the site of the old Joshua Tree.

This last one garners the most adherents, as nothing perks up people's interest like the discovery of filthy lucre or its raw materials.

Of course I know the real skinny, but Midnight Louie was not born yesterday and I learned long ago not to open my mouth except to put something edible into it.

Now it is not so surprising that speculation runs, you might say, rife around town over Mr. Nicky Fontana and this new doll. I just happen to be quietly ensconced in the lobby of the Joshua Tree the morning after her first day in town, and her first night out on the town with Mr. Nicky Fontana, when she buttonholes him right in front of the dead potted palm at 10 a.m. in the morning, West Coast time.

Mr. Nicky Fontana is engaged in ankling his way to the pool out back, which he keeps in pristine shape, as he likes nothing more than his comforts. So there he is, his long Eye-talian eyelashes still laced half shut, wearing no more than his Cardin swim trunks, which is to say not much, and a towel with "Hotel Joshua Tree" embroidered on it slung over his arm.

But Miss Van von Rhine does not seem to notice Mr. Nicky Fontana's state of casual attire, being all dressed up as if she had been out, which indeed she had been, as she is soon to reveal to him and, inadvertently, myself. She is waving around one of those pocket guides to Vegas and telling him that she wishes to see all the hotels, lock, stock, and casinos, and she would as soon get started on this admirable goal today.

Mr. Nicky Fontana, he does not say much (he is not so dumb either), but any fool can see that he has other plans for his time than squiring this doll around. But she has been to the tourist and convention bureau office, she explains, first thing, and is convinced that she needs to "study the competition," with which Mr. Nicky Fontana is in no position to argue, since it is his uncle Mario's study of the competition to which the Fontana Family owes its current prestige in certain Las Vegas circles better left unnamed.

So they go out together morning, noon, and night, which is when the word starts buzzing that something is up, and all Mr. Nicky Fontana's friends start showing up like lost puppies at the Joshua Tree, which crowds my act somewhat, but I am a generous fellow.

And every morning Mr. Nicky Fontana's eyelids hang a little heavier, but Miss Van von Rhine, she is tough stuff. He does not so much as see her wilt even after a day in 119-degree July heat pounding the Strip's sidewalks from A to C, which is the Aladdin Hotel on the south to the California Hotel at the north end of downtown.

Every once in a while he tries to make a joke of it when they come back to the Joshua Tree, but Miss Van von Rhine is not amused. Rome, she says, was not built in a day, yet he expects his hotel to be rebuilt in six months, so no time is to be wasted in checking out the competition. This is the worst thing to tell someone like Mr. Nicky Fontana, who has made wasting time into an art of high dimensions.

Like I said before, none of this is unexpected to an old Vegas hand like myself, and while some might be laying cash money down on how long it will be before Mr. Nicky Fontana runs for the airport and puts this particular kitten back on a plane for parts unknown, I keep my hand mum and play it two ways — to a straight or a royal flush.

♣ Chapter Six ♣

Van pressed her forehead against the wide, dust-spotted window of her room, studying a swath of landscape seven stories below.

Seen in daylight and from above, the city of Las Vegas, almost half a million strong, looked no more populous or impressive than a Gobi desert crossroads community.

Except for the high-rise hubris of hotels like the Landmark, the two Hiltons, the MGM Grand, the Imperial Palace and the Tropicana, it remained a lethargic, lackluster settlement of two- and three-story buildings endlessly strung out into the surrounding desert like beads on a network of naked electrical wires.

Van shook her head without lifting her forehead from the glass, which acted as a morning-cool compress on her fevered emotions. Why would anyone, she asked herself, want to live here — or want to come here, even if gambling was legal, as it was not elsewhere? So was prostitution; Van had done her research, even if it took her into sleazy corners.

Why had she been so desperate to escape the ghosts of Europe that she had taken this commission at the end of the civilized world, and in that wasteland of popular culture, her mother's native America? You can bring class to the country, she told herself, but you can't make the country classy.

Van shook herself briskly and moved away from the hypnotically barren view outside her window. As much as Mr. Fontana — Nick — irritated, confused, and unnerved her, she'd told him that she could convert a sow's ear into an

Ultrasuede purse, and by Miss Piggy, she would do it!

This morning she planned to explore — solo — the Joshua Tree from freight elevator to rooftop. Nicky had the day off.

"I probably know more about what's to be found in this hotel than you do," she'd told him airily on parting at three that morning after a sultry walking tour of Glitter Gulch downtown.

The patent relief that had flooded the blacks of his eyes had been curiously disappointing. Van was beginning to enjoy running Nicky Fontana ragged, especially since she had perceived that he found no pleasure in her company. Yet his energetically ingratiating presence sapped her composure for some nameless reason. She needed a vacation from him.

So Van, like a horse who comes to find movement a chore without the familiar irritant of a spur, forced herself down to the main floor and a survey of the hotel's less publicly glamorous regions.

She began with the kitchen, eager to meet the skeleton staff that supplied the few staff people still quartered in the Joshua Tree with their morning biscuits, afternoon tea, and an unceasing flow of Nicky Fontana's all-time anytime favorite food — hamburgers. Naturally.

So far, Van had spied only the mute Oriental waiter who brought up her breakfast. She telephoned her daily orders to an unseen someone nearly as mute as he, except for an invariably cheerful "Okey-dokey" sign-off.

When her hesitant hand swung half of the double stainless steel doors open on an area at the hotel's rear, Van paused, amazed. The kitchen sparkled in a welter of copper-bottomed pans and polished steel tables, all arrayed in such blinding order that they almost outshone the tinsel that bedecked much more public parts of more inhabited Las Vegas hotels.

"Point One to Nicky Fontana," Van murmured, impressed by the quality of the kitchen's equipment, although its vastness was mostly unpeopled.

Did elves whip up the delicate tea that appeared as if by magic on her afternoon tray? Who baked the croissants that fell into tender flakes at the slightest prodding? And the exquisitely sweet-tart plum jam blooming crimson in the tiny white porcelain bowls of saki cups, it wasn't the pre-packaged variety that came in foil pillboxes in hotels the world over.

"Hello . . . is anybody on duty?"

Only silent spit and polish answered her. Van explored her way through the suspended pots.

"I just want to say hello, ask some questions —"

She paused, mystified. An alien aroma wafted to her nostrils, then toyed further with her sense of smell. It was spicy; no, delicate! It was. . . .

On the wide institutional stove top a dented pot's unfamiliar contents churned busily. Van leaned her inquiring nose closer to the steamy vapors than was prudent. "Soup — ?" she wondered aloud.

"Wonton!" burst out the same voice that sang Van's morning "okey-dokey."

"Of course! Wonton soup. But —" Van turned. An Oriental gentleman in a green knit Izod shirt was beaming easily translated satisfaction at her.

He snatched up a ladle and a Canton soupbowl; in an instant Van was sniffing the steam rising from her personal portion of the no-longer-mysterious brew.

"No, really, I've just had breakfast — and a splendid breakfast it was," she added, immediately perceiving that she addressed no less a personage than the chef. "But I don't need any soup at the moment."

His smile didn't wilt as she set the bowl aside.

"I'd like to inquire about the hotel's food service possibilities. The kitchens seem adequate to support the three or four house restaurants we'll need. How do you feel about that assessment?"

"Okey-dokey." The chef's smile neither dimmed nor rose one watt.

Van smiled back, weakly.

"If you need . . . time . . . to marshal an opinion, or want to put it in writing —"

"Ah!" The chef nodded with sage confidence and produced a sheet of parchment, plucked up a small brush and etched a rapid series of symbols. He flourished the result at Van. "Okey-dokey," he summed up.

"Very nice," Van hedged, edging toward the stainless steel exit doors. She doubted Nicky Fontana spoke Japanese, or Chinese, or whatever dialect was required, but someone had to be able to communicate with Mr. Oki-Doki. She hated interrupting Nicky's first morning sleep-in with so basic a problem, but Van recognized when she needed help.

It came, unannounced, through another set of swinging double doors, which burst open like the winged portals to a hospital emergency room. Poised before the fluttering steel doors as they whooshed shut again was a tiny woman in black satin pajamas. Two ebony picks angled through her silver-haired topknot at a slant precisely matching the tilt of India-ink eyes.

"I am Madame Song," she announced. "I speak; Mr. Song cook. You want bird's nest soup instead of wonton, Miss?"

"No! That is, I'm sure it's excellent; everything from the kitchen since I've arrived has been superb, even the . . . um, hamburgers. But I'm not hungry now."

Chef Song's sunny expression fell, as if intuitively registering a nearby lack of appetite.

"The . . . two of you have been running the kitchens, then?" Van inquired.

"Yes." Madame Song's head nodded china-doll fashion. Her mute husband folded his arms on his chest, revealing a skindiver's watch, as he leaned against a table to watch. "We come with the hotel."

"Then you worked at the old Joshua Tree?"

She nodded briskly. "The kitchen is ours. Mr. Nicky say so. Mr. Nicky will give Mr. Song fine restaurant to run all his way when everything is new again. Mr. Song best Chinese cook in Las Vegas."

"I don't doubt it," Van said, doubting a great many other things at that moment, including "Mr. Nicky's" sanity. "So you two are alone here," she went on.

"Oh, no." Madame Song sounded as cheerful as her mono-phrased spouse looked, then clapped tiny hands. The silver doors fanned open again — and again and again and again — until a step-ladder of small Asian faces confronted Van.

"Ching chops; Kang bakes; Chien tears salad greens and Sung, Ming and Han clean up." Madame Song's hands tapped the glossy black top of each head in turn, much as if she were striking a familiar melody on a xylophone. At each touch, the round face below lit up in recognition of its introduction.

"But they seem so young. . . ."

"All Chinese children work; serve the family. And at hotel, there is a bigger family to feed. We must be busy now.

Good day, Miss. Come back for soup."

All bowed in unison, except Mr. Song, and popped through the double doors in sequence like a string of beads.

Van turned to the chef, whose stance with a meat cleaver cocked in one hand was at least familiar from her past. Before she could think of anything to say, he set her worries once more at rest.

"Okey-dokey," Mr. Song intoned sonorously, nodding farewell.

She left, following the nondescript hall to the unrehabilitated lobby, but perversely pleased to observe some neglect in contrast to the awesome, unassailably efficient occupation of the kitchen.

But the lobby was not deserted, as Van was accustomed to seeing it. A narrow man reading a tabloid occupied one of the lumpy lounge chairs. She'd noticed him hanging around the lobby before and suspected him of being an ex-bellman assigned to fetching Nicky's Corvette to the front door.

The other person, who stood and tapped an impatient foot, Van had not seen before, and clearly was better off for it.

"Can I help you?" Van began politely.

The visitor studied Van from her low-heeled sandals to the sleek apex of her French twist before she spoke.

"I hope so, honey, 'cuz I sure ain't getting anything out of Nicky lately."

At this, the nondescript man anchoring the easy chair sniggered into the close type of his periodical.

The woman drew herself up to her full height, a loftiness abetted by three-inch heels held to her instep by a curve of clear plastic embroidered with pink sequins depicting a Mexican market scene.

"That is to say," she added pointedly, seemingly for the

benefit of the anonymous gentleman who was doing nothing to avoid overhearing them, "I have been unable to contact Mr. Fontana of late."

Van smiled. "Mr. Fontana has been out late — of late," she purred.

The woman tossed her long hair, gathered into a scarf high enough on her sorrel-colored head to remind Van of a horse's tail.

"I don't imagine you have anything to say about who — um Mr. Fontana sees, even if you may know something of his movements. So I shall go up unannounced."

The prospect of seeing Nicky Fontana awakened beforetimes by this tiger lily of a woman was too much, even for Van's innate restraint.

"You may go up unannounced, surely, but I'll be right along myself. I have some questions about the hotel staffing that only . . . Mr. Fontana . . . can answer."

"Then Mr. Fontana has a lot to answer for this morning." The woman's narrowed eyes studied Van.

Van studied her baldly back, being far too intrigued by the woman's mode of dress to resist. Her sundress, an explosive peach, orange and pink floral pattern, featured innumerable cutouts through which her white flesh peeped frankly. Said cutouts seemed to be arranged solely to demonstrate the impossibility of its wearer donning any conventional undergarments.

Impressed, Van tried to count them, but lost her place when the woman's contact-lens-intensified green eyes flashed and she intoned direly, "I am Roxelle, an old and dear friend of Mr. Fontana's. And you must be —" She waited, implacable.

"Van von Rhine, the hotel manager." Van extended her own pale hand.

"How do you do," the giantess said carefully. Painted nails as long as caviar knives pressed Van's palm. Van tightened her clasp despite this strong disincentive and smiled even more serenely.

"Please go right up, Miss . . . Roxelle. I'll be along presently."

"You can come up later," Roxelle said defiantly.

"That's what I meant. I'm afraid I don't speak Las Vegas-ese fluently yet."

" 'Las Vegas-ese!' That's rich." Roxelle's laugh was predictably throaty. "Listen, honey; the secret to life in Las Vegas is written right in the word itself; it's a gas!"

Roxelle kicked up her interesting heels and departed with enough clicking to imitate Western Union. Her parting wave of horsey laughter was echoed by the little man now burying his mirth in the paper covering his face.

"I don't believe that we've been introduced." Van hovered over him, in no mood to be put off.

He jackknifed to his feet, his head coming only to Van's chin. This contrast of uncalled-for tall and surprisingly short was beginning to make Van feel like a suddenly shrinking and expanding Alice in Wonderland.

"Greetings to the lady who comes from o'er the sea," the fellow responded, bowing. "Who's come to Las Vegas to save the Joshua Tree."

"Is that your name too — Joshua Tree?" Van found herself teasing. The man looked like he could stand some saving, especially with the race track tipsheet folded under his arm.

His eyes lit up under a black thicket of eyebrows. "Alas, dear lady, I fear it is not. But just think if it were . . . how I'd not be forgot."

"If I wanted to forget you," Van interrogated severely,

"what name would I strike from my consciousness?"

"The name, fair inquisitor, is Nostradamus; I'm known in this town, although not famous."

"More infah-mous, I'd think. I imagine you, too, would like to see Mr. Fontana. I'm not his secretary, you know."

"Mr. Fontana can wait 'til tomorrow. He'd only want something I ain't got to borrow."

"Did . . . did Indian Summer win the other day?" Van asked.

"Ah, the lady has a mem'ry and no excusin'. That's one nag that gives Nostradamus a bruisin'."

"Then if you owe Nicky and are in no hurry," Van responded absently, "you can see him tomorrow, and not to worry." She froze, aware of what she'd just done.

Nostradamus grinned, exposing amiably crooked teeth.

"I'd be pleased to eschew the lovely Roxelle," he added, backing away like a courtier. "She seemed in a mood for the dispensing of hell."

"Curiouser and curiouser," Van murmured as the man merged with the hot blot of sunlight beyond the hotel's glassed entry doors, and vanished.

She understood why the lobby attracted a motley group of loiterers. It was quiet, cool and — God knew — distinctly uncrowded, unlike the frenetic lobbies of operational Las Vegas hotels. For a wild moment she contemplated capitalizing on the Joshua Tree's air of genteel neglect. She could rename it the "Lost Silver Slipper," line the lobby with slot machines, forego redecorating and probably make a mint.

Van shook that reverie loose and marched for the penthouse elevator. She hoped Miss Roxelle was as adept at the giving of hell as she was at walking on her ridiculously high heels. Nicky Fontana could use some hellfire.

But as the elevator door hushed open on the empty hall

of the thirteenth floor, Van paused. Thirteen, she thought darkly. What a foolhardy way to cap off a hotel! No wonder the place had suffered a fire during the unfortunate rash of hotel blazes a few years back, she thought. She must convince Nicky that safety first, glitz second should be their operating motto.

Van paused by the numberless door to which Mr. Maxwell had introduced her last week. She hadn't been here since and wondered what she was doing here now. Certainly she had things to discuss with the man behind the closed door; just as certainly she didn't have to broach him now, when he had . . . company.

Indecipherable voices ebbed and flowed behind the door, reminding Van of whole hallways of closed hotel doors, of hotel after hotel with doors always closed and mysterious adult business transpiring behind their bland facades. For an instant she became again that only, lonely child of six or ten or thirteen who called a house of hundreds of bedrooms home and considered doormen and desk clerks playmates. She studied the blank door until it became one of legion.

Her own father had often disappeared behind just such a door, commending his young daughter to the care of a nearby employee as he escorted a tall (but everyone had seemed tall to a child), dark-garbed woman with glittering eyes and begemmed throat and hands behind a door.

At such times Van's instructions were clear: Such closed doors must never be tested, not even if a nightmare came to take the young dreamer on a wild ride. And hotels were full of closed doors.

"My Vanilla's a big girl now," Erick von Rhine would tease her uneasily. "She's the Princess of the Ritz" — or the Hilton or the Stattler, depending on which hotel in what country her father managed at the moment. He had been a handsome, tall blond man as disciplined as a broom handle. Later, a more worldly wise Van understood why the jewelry-decked ladies had so discreetly come and gone in her father's rooms.

By then she had been old enough to excuse him; her mother had died when Van was an infant, after all. Her mother had been American — and whimsical, Nanny had told Van once. Althea von Rhine had perpetrated the "Vanilla," a first name that seemed to embarrass her dignified father, and eventually came to embarrass its holder.

So when Van turned sixteen and announced that hereafter she would be "Van," no paternal voice countermanded this teen-age act of rebellion, if indeed it was such. It was Van's sole self-assertion throughout the luxe nomadic life she shared with her father.

His sudden death by heart attack happened behind a closed door, too. Van suspected that one of the tall, dark, dimly glittering ladies had been discreetly hurried from the scene by the assistant manager.

But it was the closed doors she resented — not the death that had finally checked in behind one of them. She resented the men behind them with their secrets not suitable for a girl of tender years, the women who smiled down at her tolerantly in passing and who always called her "Vanilla" as if amused. It was the act of being shut out she minded most.

So now she challenged another door, unsure why; a closed door she had no personal right to question, except for the excuse of business and a niggling bit of malicious curiosity.

Van's hands had become fists at her side during her brief mental journey back in time. She lifted her right one in the present and rapped sharply on the closed, unnumbered door.

♣ Chapter Seven ♣

"Yeah?" Nicky Fontana's voice shouted.

"Van von Rhine," she shot back.

"Come in," he called promptly.

Van turned the knob and pushed the door into the room.

Its interior landscape had changed since the previous week; more flotsam than ever floated in its wide open spaces. Nicky sprawled on a zebra-print loveseat, three unsmoked but crushed cigarettes screwed into the ashtray in front of him. A pristine fourth danced in his nervous fingers.

Obviously, Roxelle's unannounced arrival had hauled him from the shower. His wet hair coiled like ebony rigatoni. Waterdrops dewed bare shoulders. Wearing only trousers and with a rolled hand towel around his neck, Nicky glanced up at Van like a punchy prizefighter trapped in his corner between rounds nine and ten.

His sullenly percolating eyes didn't broadcast the emotion Van had anticipated — anger, irritation or dismissal. Instead, they poured out a relief as frankly naked as Nicky himself.

She stared at him, stunned. Was that what lurked behind all those faceless shut doors — welcome, if only she had tried them sooner? Closed doors all along the corridor of Van's mind sprung a surprised half-inch open.

She turned to the woman pacing impatiently in front of the mirrored bar. Roxelle's striding figure fumed in triplicate, each reflection smaller than the last. The more Roxelle made of herself, the less she seemed to matter.

"This was a private conversation," Roxelle huffed out.

"Me and Nicky have to get a few things settled about how much time this hotel thing is going to take from our personal . . . relationship."

"I see," Van said sagely. "And what is that relationship — kissing cousins?"

Nicky concealed his sudden grin by dabbing his upper lip with the towel.

"Something like that. Anyway, Miss von Ryan, you should know that daytimes are the only few precious hours we have together. Your demands on Nicky's time are most inconvenient."

"I don't see why. I take him out mostly at night."

"You do! He swore he hardly had anything to do with you! At all! Anytime!"

Roxelle's impressive heels took a wide, combative stance as her fists punctuated her hips. All she needed was a feather boa laced through her akimbo arms to present a picture-perfect representation of a floozy. Fortunately, the patently obvious escaped Roxelle.

"Furthermore," she went on, "I expect things to get back to normal pretty darn soon! Danny Dove says my nervous excitement shows in my dancing."

"Who is Danny Dove?" Van couldn't resist asking.

The long whip of ponytail tossed to further clarify Roxelle's position. "My choreographer. I am a lead dancer in the 'Lido' revue and personal upsets affect my performance. Isn't that right, Nicky?"

"Funny," Van said in a musing tone. " 'Nicky' was just saying that very thing the other evening."

"Well! I never!" Thinking for a moment and not unearthing exactly what she "never," Roxelle stalked to the door. "Perhaps if it's your duty to show Miss von Ryan so much of Vegas, Nicky, you could bring her over to the

Stardust to see what real Las Vegas floor-show fireworks look like."

"I don't think that'll be necessary, do you, Nicky?" Van speculated sweetly. "I think I've had a pretty good floor sample right here and now."

Slam! Van faced a closed door again, only this time, she stood inside instead of outside it. A white dart hurled to the door's wooden surface, then fell to the carpet — Nicky's last cigarette, still unsmoked despite provocation.

"Dames," he complained. "She doesn't get that this hotel is important!"

Van turned to him, expecting to share in the abuse now being accorded her sex. Instead, his look turned wry. "And what's this 'Nicky' business all of a sudden, von Rhine?"

"It seemed the thing most likely to drive her away. Besides, I give up! You can't make a Ritz out of a Holiday Inn. I guess you were born to be a Nicky."

Bare sun-browned arms stretched wide in a gesture either inviting embrace or proffering self-display. "That's me — no class, right?" Nicky summed up good-naturedly. "I know it and now you know it. So you're just going to have to beat some into me."

Van smiled skeptically. Nicky Fontana exhibited many valuable characteristics other than class — youth, energy, and an attractively sculpted masculine body that she was trying to disregard as unselfconsciously as its owner did.

He jumped up, mistaking her hesitation for discouragement.

"Cheer up; the hotel'll come together." His hands clenched shut on her bare upper arms as if to press reassurance into her or squeeze some hidden confidence out. "Hey. . . ." He shook her playfully, admonishingly. "You feel cold. I'll turn the air down. Now what was so urgent?"

It was easier to address his back as he fiddled with the thermostat across the room. Van cleared her throat and assumed a task-taking tone.

"I've just come from the kitchens, where I met Chef Song. And family."

"Oh, yeah, great cook. Great guy, but he doesn't speak much English. Aren't those kids a gas? Greased lightning with a chopping cleaver, too."

"They're perfectly wonderful, all of them. But they seem to be living in that kitchen, and Chef Song's wife says you've promised to let them run the new hotel restaurants! How can you make a commitment like that when you didn't even consult me?"

"Sing's the best Chinese chef in the city; he's an asset, it's as simple as that."

"I wouldn't care if he were Escoffier," Van began in high, righteous dudgeon. She stopped to giggle suddenly. "Did you say . . . his first name was — Sing? Sing Song? Oh, Nicky, you and your crazy hotel will be the death of sanity on this earth!"

He had turned and was laughing, too. "Yeah, and the kids are all named after dynasties — Ching Song, Chien Song, Han Song —"

"— Ming Song, Kang Song and . . . and Sung Song," Van finished, collapsing hysterically on the zebra loveseat and clutching the rolled arm as if to throttle the fabric into guffawing with her. "They're out of a book for a musical — *Flower Drum Song*. Song!" She was off again. "Wherever did you find them?"

"I inherited them," Nicky explained, perching on the sofa arm to dislodge a fresh cigarette from the open pack on the coffee table. He tamped the end absently on his lighter as he spoke.

"It's not dumb to have a Chinese head chef in Vegas, you know. Oriental food's the panda's pajamas in this town; after all, Chinese immigrants came here in the eighteen-hundreds to build the railroad and stayed on. And nowadays most of our heavy high rollers are from the Near and Far East. Chef Song was one of 'em himself once."

"A chef?"

"Sing was a millionaire Hong Kong export king; used to bet hundreds of thousands, and he always brought his family along. The hotels fell over themselves giving him their best suites — free, like they do for certified high rollers with extensive credit. You see, when the Japanese come over to the states to gamble, they travel in groups of dudes; the Chinese are domestic types; they always bring their families.

"So when Sing lost his whole wad — which is to say a good percent of Hong Kong — he had nowhere to go back to and no way to pay." The unlit cigarette floated rhythmically to Nicky's savoring lips as he talked. "The old Joshua Tree management was going to sue, but they went under. When I took over I said — by way of Mrs. Song — 'Sing, you're a first-rate chef, so you can work off your debt cooking at this new hotel I'm gonna make out of the old one.' That's the story."

Nicky finished his recital by stubbing out the cigarette as if he had consumed it while talking.

Crazy, Van thought, they're all crazy. She was sitting here with a half-naked man who pretended to smoke cigarettes and ran a hotel on high hopes and a soft heart. Who was to say Sing Song was not the sanest of them all? At least he had exited the rat race to retreat to a peaceful kitchen island, thanks to one last unlucky roll of the dice or turn of the cards.

"Communicating with him will be hard," Van mused.

"He doesn't speak much English."

Nicky shrugged.

"He's a bit old to learn something as foreign to him as English," he explained. "But Mrs. Song knows chapter and verse of how to get what she wants in Chinese and English, and a few Anglo cuss words, too. She's one shrewd fortune cookie. The only thing she couldn't do was curb the old man's gambling fever."

"I'm not saying the Song family isn't competent, or even that they shouldn't have a Chinese restaurant in our hotel," Van added, "but you can't go on making unilateral commitments regarding the running of it, Nicky. We have to plan the new hotel cooperatively."

Nicky's nervous fingers stretched for another cigarette, then paused. Instead, they snatched Van's hand from the sofa arm and sandwiched it within their encompassing warmth.

" 'Our hotel.' Say, does that mean you'll stick it out; that you'll give it a shot? Hell, does that mean you give a damn?"

Van stared into the intensity of his eyes, as consuming as the infamous black holes of space that absorb all matter into their bottomless depths. She wet her lips and then regretted it when his eyes automatically flicked to the gesture.

"I wouldn't put it quite that way —" she began.

"No, you wouldn't," he said, amused.

"But I don't like to give up."

"Me neither," he said ardently. "Now that you call me 'Nicky,' how about telling me your real name?"

"It's Van."

"No, it's not. Nobody'd name a cotton-candy baby like you after a light-duty truck. . . . Maybe it's Lily — Lily-of-the-valley. Las Vegas is in a valley, you know."

He seemed to be leaning closer, although neither of them

had moved. Van became instantly aware of the delicate perfume she applied routinely every morning rising newly fragrant from a surge of inner heat at all her pulse points.

"That comes in a bottle," she said, withdrawing her hand.

"And you don't." He laughed and rose to pace away in his own patented version of perpetual motion. "Okay. We work together on 'our hotel.' But warning's fair —"

She froze, every capillary constricting in anticipation of his next words.

"— I'm going to find out what you're hiding behind those three little letters of your first name." An admonitory finger shook her way as she laughed in free-floating relief.

"Do your worst! If that's all you can threaten me with, the Fontana Family must be losing its grip."

His expression hardened. "I'm not the Family. I'm me — solo. Don't forget that, Van. It's important to me, maybe as important as your real name is to you."

She nodded, then stood to go.

"What are your plans today?" he wanted to know.

"To see more of the hotel."

"Why don't you relax for a few hours?" Nicky cajoled, leading her to the door. "Take a dip in the pool, lie in the sun — hey, you've practically got the joint to yourself. Then we'll go out tonight — final tour. But no pressure like on one of your usual white-glove inspections. You've got to amble to gamble. So we'll hit a few casinos and maybe end up at the Goliath. There are some things there you gotta see to believe."

"Not as many as there are here," Van observed on the threshold. Nicky was close behind her, the brush of his hands on her shoulders guiding her out.

She advanced far into the hall before turning. He had arranged himself casually in the doorway, as if recognizing her need to separate from him. Behind him the pale door gaped open, a bland background for the earthy shade and symmetry of his form.

"Ciao," Nicky said softly, smiling and patting his still-damp hair with the towel edge.

To Van it sounded like "goodbye" when it's intended to imply "hello."

Van nodded uncertainly at another nondescript little man of late middle age staking out a spot in the empty lobby. The hotel crawled with anonymous casual visitors, yet each time she questioned one's right to be there, she found a Nostradamus or a Roxelle or some other acquaintance of Nicky's.

Now she ignored them all, although — having taken Nicky's advice about what she would do for once — he felt a bit nonplused about parading her silky high-cut French maillot swimsuit past a strange man.

But once at the hotel's rear, Van's bare feet slowed. It felt wonderful to slip quietly away to a private pool carrying nothing but a hotel towel and a tube of sunscreen lotion. She studied the surroundings, her managerial mind toting up substandard features and visualizing improvements.

The hotel was hourglass shaped — a broad curve of lobby, restaurant, and casino up front narrowed to a shopping arcade passage and then flared wide again to curved wings of guest floors. Nestled at the rear between the building's embracing white stucco arms, a blue rectangle of pool glistened like a giant emerald-cut aquamarine drying in the sun.

Van sighed relief to see the Mediterranean-style courtyard, with its palm fans scouring the cobalt Las Vegas sky. White patio furniture gleamed clean against green oddments of well-tended lawn.

Within the building's shadow grew a stand of sunset-hued canna lilies as tall as she. An Oriental rock garden rambled over stone-formed hills; silver threads of water crisscrossed until massing into a still pond.

Van's breath eased out as if she were expelling every last bit of it for the first time since arriving in this flat arid city of artificially lit nights and burned-out days. Here, against the sheltering shade of the hotel walls, unsuspected beauty whispered its secrets.

Something dimpled the pool's dark surface — a gold glitter uncheapened by sunlight, rich and elusive. Van leaned down to see a pirate's ransom of scaled gold writhing beneath the watery wine-dark surface — carp, not the plain-Jane variety that populate large bodies of public water like Lake Mead, but the enamel-bright schools of showy fish that ornament private ponds.

Van, hands on her bare knees, bent to watch them. An airy scarf of sensation drifted past her ankles. She jumped back to see a boa of black fur wreathe her knees.

"Why, what are you doing here — ?"

The creature that had silently approached from behind looked up with noncommittal eyes of jade green. A cat, Van realized. The biggest, fattest, blackest feline Van had ever seen. Snow-white whiskers sprayed from above its eyes and bracketed its all-black nose. Its mute meow showed teeth as white, profuse and pointed as whisker barbs.

"Aren't you handsome?" Van's admiration was interrupted by a rustle among the tall canna lily leaves.

A pair of ebony hunter's eyes peered out. Before she could react, a muscular figure bounded onto the stones beside her. The broad rectangular silver of a meat cleaver flashed as preciously as the golden fish still swirling at Van's feet.

Chef Sing Song, unreeling strings of Chinese imprecations with awesome fluidity, slashed expertly at the outsized cat.

"Chef Song!" For an instant Van's tone and address, perhaps reminiscent of Mrs. Song's, gave him pause.

Then he shook off the interruption and darted after the cat, which skittered a few feet away and then stopped. Apparently it was not unduly alarmed by Chef Song's display of martial art, Van surmised, and apparently cat-stalking was not an unheard-of hobby of the chef's.

Van planted herself between cat and man. Both crouched — the one behind her sweeping his magnificent black tail from side to side on the stones; the one before her, his knees and meat cleaver cocked, balked but not beaten.

"No, Chef Song!" Van ordered with the firmness of Anna addressing the King of Siam. "This is merely a stray cat."

A low growl of protest issued from behind her, but Van didn't dare remove her eyes from the bloodthirsty chef.

"Why would you want to hurt it? You don't . . . that is, we don't —" An appalling thought about certain Asian eating habits involving birds, fish, snakes and dogs hovered. Were cats also included? Van resolved never to order another hamburger from the kitchen.

But Chef Song continued to exercise his native tongue, pointing with great umbrage to the roiling pond — for even the fish had sensed the uproar — then flourishing his cleaver with a zealot's enthusiasm.

"There will be no cats killed on the grounds of this hotel," Van insisted, "even if it . . . accosts the goldfish.

Please, Chef Song, return to your kitchen." She pointed sweepingly, almost touching the poised blade.

This heroic stance perhaps revived a memory of Madam Song. His face assumed an expression of sullen defeat. With one last glare at the animal sheltering behind Van's legs, he lowered his cleaver and stalked back into the hotel.

"Oh, poor kitty," she crooned to her protégé, bending to lift its heavy body, which oozed down toward the stones like Silly Putty caught by sheer gravity. Still, its eyes had a lean and hungry look. Van slipped back into the hotel kitchen, snatching a soup bowl and some milk from under Chef Song's disapproving nose, eyes, and meat cleaver, and rushed back to the pool.

The animal had waited for her, as instructed, settling somewhat nearer the forbidden carp pond. Van nudged it away to set the milk down. It regarded her with a slightly defrauded expression, then lowered its head to lick milk until a swashbuckling moustache of white further bleached its midnight countenance.

Van crouched happily beside it. "Oh, but aren't you a beauty!" she said, smoothing the cat's head. Hotel cats, Van's only pets, were considered a source of amusement and good luck at most European establishments. Even her father had tolerated a "house" cat or two.

But not black ones, Van thought, rising slowly to avoid disturbing the cat's drinking. Black cats were universally unlucky, she believed in her bones, even as she pitied any creature forced to eke a living from the dry stones of a desert city.

So . . . Van edged carefully around the blot of luxuriant black fur shading the patio stones. It hadn't yet crossed her path; perhaps it would move on to a more occupied hotel.

On that hope she stepped into the searing sunlight. The

dry, intense heat lowered her habitual sense of unease here in this hotel another discernable notch. Feeling as if she moved in a sauna, she dropped her towel by the pool's deep end and sheathed herself in a cool, blue-silk sari of water as she dove.

Later, Van chose one of perhaps seventy empty lounge chairs, applied sun lotion, and lay back. The world beyond the Strip's near, noise-ridden fringes was silent, a place of soft wind slowly drying the waterdrops dewing her parched skin. She could almost hear bees buzzing in the nearby bushes — large bees — very large bees!

Van sat up, alarm opening her eyes. Sound thrummed all around her, but the air was empty. Finally, in the shadow her lounge chair made, she spied the vibration's source. The cat, motionless and black as cast iron, was taking an after-milk nap under her chair.

She tiptoed away. Waking the cat would only encourage it to cross her path. She went slowly, looking back, and walked straight into a pillar that hadn't been there before — a sun-warmed bronzed column in the Italian style, composed of firm bare flesh. Nicky Fontana in swimtrunks.

"Oh!" Van clutched her towel to her air-dried suit. *Rotten luck already!* she thought.

"No harm done." Nicky's hold on her arms kept her from sidling past him. "I'm glad you took my advice. But I don't recall prescribing a dish of milk."

She glanced at the near-empty bowl near the carp pond.

"For the cat." She nodded over her shoulder, looking back to find Nicky studying the shrug of that shoulder, as bare as his now and a good deal whiter. Of all people to be caught seminaked by, Van fussed mentally. She wouldn't make that mistake again.

"I wouldn't do that again," Nicky said gravely.

"W-what?" she squeaked, confused. Did black cats cause mind reading too?

"I wouldn't give that jaded old tomcat plain milk. He likes a little Scotch in it — or rather, a little milk in his hooch."

"You know the cat?"

"He's a neighborhood layabout. Sing's been trying to make him into fricassee of feline for months. The black devil keeps putting his big paws into Sing's special stash of goldfish."

"Oh, that's why —"

"Why what?" Nicky had finally released her and now did something worse. He stepped back, which gave him a Cinemascopic view of her figure.

Van moved her towel to her shoulder, pretending to pat at long-gone beads of water. "— why Chef Song was brandishing a meat cleaver," she said. "I thought he'd kill the creature before my eyes. I could barely convince him to return to the kitchen."

Traitorously, Van's eyes dallied on the pleasing sun-and-shadow-shaped contours of Nicky's swim-suited form. In the muffler of shadow the high-noon sun cast around his throat, a gold charm glittered hypnotically. Even his eyelashes, luxuriously long enough to add mystery to his angular face, threw tiny fringed shadows of themselves on his slanted cheekbones. Clothed, Nicky seemed hirsute enough to please King Kong; unclothed, his hairless, statue-smooth chest struck Van as oddly vulnerable, intriguingly tactile . . . She made her roving eyes focus on the greenery behind Nicky.

"You faced off Chef Song on the warpath?" Nicky was saying, his fever-dark eyes squinting good-humoredly in the sunshine. "Good for you! I wouldn't try it." He laughed, flashing teeth as white as the cat's, if less pointed.

Now that the neck-hung towel was gone, Van could finally see that the charm at his neck dangled from a thick gold chain, the kind that certain male entertainers who favor open-necked shirts liked to nestle in their copious chest hair. The gold, revealed to be common, after all, shone garishly against the smooth swell of tanned muscles as hairless as those carved into Michelangelo's *David*. Van supposed that was less vulgar at least.

"How do you like it?" Nicky was asking with a grin that seemed knowing.

"What?" she asked back, appalled, wringing her hands tighter on the towel clutched to her breastbone.

"The grotto." Nicky gestured, his eyes finally leaving her for the scenery. "I thought I'd . . . we . . . could keep it like this. Sing wants to keep the fish and it seems peaceful here."

"Very peaceful," Van said enthusiastically. "Most refreshing! I wouldn't change a thing about it — not a thing." She brushed past him to slip through the tinted glass door into the hallway beyond.

Nicky turned to observe her sudden departure, his face openly puzzled. Van, safe behind the tinted glass, allowed herself one last look at what had seemed an idyllically private retreat, then plunged back into the safety of the hotel's semideserted shadow.

By the time she reached her floor her heart had stopped pounding as if she had been running for her life. She followed the hall to the single window at its end. Seven floors below, Nicky Fontana was a lithe mahogany toothpick hurling itself onto a sky-blue lacquer tray.

She watched him dive, striking water with speed enough to make her catch the useless towel to her throat again. There was no one else there — no one — except . . . From beneath the lounge chair that had been hers, Van could have sworn a pair of solemn green eyes were gazing precisely at the window where she stood.

She whirled away from her looking post and found a tall, faint figure staring at her from far down the hall. Van froze. Most of the hotel workers quartered on the floor were working at this mid-day hour — and, besides, their rooms were far enough from hers that she seldom saw them come and go.

He seemed an older man. Van couldn't say why, except his posture seemed slightly stooped and his hair gleamed vaguely silver, almost like a halo. For a bizarre moment she thought she saw the ghost of her father at an age he had never lived to enjoy . . . her father in his seventies passing through the hall of some hotel he had managed once. Perhaps he did — somewhere. But not here, not in her hotel. . . .

The man melted into one of the doors that distance had foreshortened into an anonymous muddle. If Van raced down the corridor to find it, she couldn't be sure which one it had been. It was near her own door, that she knew. She shivered in the full-blast air-conditioning. First a fat black cat. Now a thin silver man.

The thought of Nicky Fontana coming to her room in a few hours, of Nicky Fontana and herself moving back into the heated, frantic wave of Las Vegas nightlife, was no longer unpleasant. She could use some company right now, Van thought with sudden, humbling insight — any company.

♣ Chapter Eight ♣

"So what do you think?"

"I don't know what to say," Van said quite honestly.

Above Van and Nicky loomed the limitless black Las Vegas night sky and the gargantuan thighs of a plaster figure whose dimensions dwarfed even those of Michelangelo's *David*.

It was, of course, Goliath. The several-story-high figure of a man straddling the hotel entrance at least wore a kilt, knee-high leather-strapped sandals . . . and neon bulbs that twinkled as ribaldly as the expression looming high above them.

Nicky guided Van under the anthropomorphic archway while she fought an irresistible impulse to look up. How had they managed to get around that? At least one couldn't stroll beneath the ersatz *David* at Caesars Palace, she thought with relief.

"This is the biggest sign on the Strip," Nicky was explaining, "taller even than the Dune's minaret, and that's twenty-two stories. It's based on some ancient Wonder of the World — the giant . . . no, the Colossus of Rhodes, that's it! This place has got it all," Nicky promised happily while Van mentally inscribed "Abandon taste, all ye who enter here" on Goliath's flashing belt buckle.

Barely had the statue ebbed into their wake, when they confronted the hotel marquee — a wrap-around Philistine banquet scene. Wavering neon made the figures seem endlessly caught in mid-orgy.

"Now, this is a little flashy," Nicky cautioned sotto voce.

He escorted Van through the dark-tinted revolving doors by slipping them both into one slot and ushering her through in the close custody of his arm.

Inside the Goliath, icy air and darkness — a complete reversal of the Strip's daylight-bright, overheated nighttime extravagance — momentarily blinded Van. She blinked in the shelter of Nicky's shoulder, letting her ears take in the rush of voices, the brittle clink of coins and bar glasses, until her eyes adjusted to the deliberately dim nightscape of a Las Vegas casino.

While she attempted to focus, a dancing girl attired in seven mysteriously attached veils shimmied past with a full tray of equally miraculously poised cocktails. Girls dispensing ready change chimed past wearing coin-strung bikinis and trailing gaudy veils like the visible fumes of cheap perfume.

"Now this is something!" Nicky said, surveying the crowd.

"Yes," Van agreed weakly, wondering why she'd bothered putting on her classy midnight-blue dress for this latest visit to a den of decorative iniquity. "Could we . . . could I sit down, please?"

Eager to impress her, Nicky squired her up some steps covered in coagulated red carpeting into a murky cocktail lounge. There, sunk onto a rug-covered divan, Van dug her high heels into the mushy carpeting for balance and studied the gilt camel-saddle-cum-cocktail table for a spot to place her evening bag.

She stared bemused at the drink menu when a slave girl in gold lamé dropped it off.

"Stay away from the 'Rhodes Map,' " Nicky urged solicitously. "I want you to really see this place, and that drink's guaranteed to make your eyeballs look like sixteen state highways ran across 'em."

"I think," Van said without thinking, "I'll try the . . . 'Philistine Sling.' "

Across the saddle, Nicky winced. "That Sling can really knock you out," he warned.

Van frowned her indecision. "The . . . uh . . . Vizier's Revenge, I guess —"

The waitress nodded and danced away.

Van laid down her menu and the law when they were alone again. "No cutesy names for drinks at the Joshua Tree, all right?"

"Maybe." Nicky squirmed on the mushy divan. "But that's what people like about this town. It's fun."

"Bad taste is not fun."

"Says who?" Nicky's voice had risen a little, perhaps in answer to the racket all around them.

His open-necked ivory silk shirt set off the gold neck charm he wore. Van wished that something so inherently flashy didn't look so seductively appropriate. Nicky pulled out a cigarette, regarded it wistfully for a long moment, then focused his dark eyes defiantly on hers and jammed it back in its case.

"All right," Nicky began. They leaned away from the camel saddle in concert as the waitress wiggled between them to deposit two high-rise drinks upon it. "We'll discuss fine points later. But we should find something else to call our hotel besides the Joshua Tree. That's past."

"Have you any ideas?"

"No . . ." Nicky looked as innocent as a four-year-old at a soda fountain as he sipped on the straw impaled in an exotic froth of blue-green foam christened a Kirschmet. "I just want a name that fits the Vegas, uh, ambiance. You know, glamorous. Something with a ring to it, like . . . Sahara, Riviera, Tropicana —"

"Or Fontana?" Van finished shrewdly.

Nicky sputtered into his straw. "Now that you mention it, why not? That doesn't sound so bad."

"Nicky." Van had taken three long slugs of the citrus-colored libation before her, which appeared to combine every liquor known to bartender into one goblet. "I frankly don't care what you call the hotel as long as its theme, presentation and renovation stay within the bounds of good taste."

"And what is that? What you say it is?"

"Perhaps," she replied primly. "Surely you don't admire this?" Her waving hand indicated a scene vaguely reminiscent of some hellishly lit Last Judgment. "Every hotel in this town is red-and-black, flocked and gilded, crystal-hung and marbleized, neon-lit and overdraped and — frankly — tacky to its toenails."

They both glanced down as their waitress flourished past, her sandaled feet displaying lime-painted nails.

"Okay." Nicky stirred on his low divan. "So things are a little . . . loud. I meant we should look the Goliath over for ideas we could, uh, translate."

"With class."

"With class, sure. That's what I pay you for, right?"

"Right," Van said grimly, planting her palms to push herself up from her seat. It didn't work. Nicky twisted himself out of his cushion first and offered a helping hand.

Once vertical again, they glared at each other.

"This seating is not designed with a view to guest comfort," Van noted.

"Maybe comfort isn't everything! I don't want one of your damn bland white hotels, that's for sure. That wouldn't work in Vegas."

"Perhaps that's because it has class!"

Nicky's fists jammed into his pockets as if to restrain themselves from less legal activities — homicide, for instance. "Maybe we'd better skip eating here; you wouldn't find it very appetizing."

"Is there anything else you wanted to show me?" Van inquired with excessive politeness.

"Yeah."

She followed him through the cavelike casino. Both of them ignored the excitement milling around the crap tables, a routine reaction for Van and a most abnormal one for Nicky.

"Come on," someone implored as they passed. "Give me seven!"

Van shuddered. Unlucky number, seven. Ahead of them another cocktail lounge flowed into an adjoining blackness lit by tiny fairy lights in potted trees. Here Nicky paused.

"This is . . . attractive," Van conceded.

"Yeah, and look at this." Encouraged, he led her to a miniature gondola upholstered in the ever-present red velvet outlined with gilt braid.

The boat rocked gently in the dark water of a canal perhaps twelve feet wide that meandered among the cocktail tables. Once Nicky had helped her into the facing seat, some mechanism propelled them oarless into midwater. Their gondola glided barge-silent past the shoreside tables.

"Pretty neat, huh?" Nicky said happily.

"But what's the point?" Van asked in a bit. "An internal canal must cost a fortune, and while the tree lights are pretty, we could see them as well from the cocktail area. Besides, gondolas hardly fit the Goliath's biblical desert theme."

"But this is a modern attraction. It's called — are you ready? — the Loh-uv-ve Moat." He coated the title in announcerlike ooze.

Van stared blankly at the tree-shadowed image of Nicky opposite her. "The Love Moat?"

"Yeah, there's this TV show here —"

"They run *The Love Boat* in Europe too; I just don't know why anyone would want to ride this silly machine through the ill-lit rear of a hotel lobby. And I really can't see —"

The gondola sallied forth silently into the dark mouth of an unseen overhang. Even the faint twinkle of fairy lights winked out. They floated in absolute dark and complete silence. After a long moment, Van's voice resumed.

"If one wished to go to a carnival midway, one would go there, not a hotel. I really can't see why anyone in his right mind would want to —"

The darkness opposite Van rustled violently. Hands seized her, reaching from the cold blackness to pull her abruptly across the small vessel, pressing her into Nicky's arms, rocking the boat, making waves. The lapping water sounded as if it was *tsking* softly at the gondola's gilded sides.

Van wasn't afraid, simply utterly startled to find Nicky Fontana's lips unerringly meeting hers in the dark. His belt buckle jabbed into her ribs. His fingers on the back of her head combed into her French twist. His lips stole her breath and his mouth plumbed the surprised depths of hers. It was a kiss right out of a movie, long and intimate and madly passionate. Or passionately angry.

"That," his voice underlined near at hand, "that is why anyone would like something as stupid as this!"

She realized that he had stopped kissing her and blinked her eyes open. The darkness had been hers, apparently for some time. A silver-haired couple at a canal-side table was eyeing them curiously as fairy lights again illuminated the inside of the gaudy little boat.

Van's evening bag lay glittering forlornly in the gondola bottom, where it had dropped when . . .

Nicky was bending to retrieve it and plunked it ungraciously in her lap, not looking at her. Van smoothed her hair and straightened her legs. Bolting back to her side of the boat would only worsen matters.

Avoiding each other's eyes, Van and Nicky waited for the gondola to glide dockside. Each managed to disembark without touching the other.

Nicky plunged ahead through the crowded tables to where the vista opened to display a casino operating at full, Saturday-night fervor. He jammed his hands into his pockets and spoke quietly without turning to her.

"It's no use. You don't dig Vegas, and even if the hotel does need class, it needs some down-to-earth pizzazz too. The Goliath may be crass, but it's always booked to the gills, and I know numbers, even if I don't know from class. It'd never work," he muttered, "us working together. I'll pay you a few grand severance money. You can go back to your fancy continental joints, and I'll put the Fontana together my way."

"You can't!" Van burst out without thinking.

"You don't know what I can or can't do." He finally turned fiery eyes on her. "Maybe I don't either, but I can try. What I can't do is work with a wet blanket!" His eyes cooled. "You don't understand Vegas, which maybe would be all right — but you don't understand me, and that's not all right. I'm not a fool."

She nodded her head. "I know that, and I know Las Vegas is built on . . . well, exaggeration. But you don't want the Goliath, Nicky. I know you well enough to know that. I'm sorry if I don't know how to react to this town, to you

. . . but I do want the Fontana to work as much as you do."

"You want to stay?"

She couldn't quite agree to that. "I need a job," she said quietly. "And, I suppose, I could stand to learn a thing or two. If you'd teach me."

"About what?" he asked dubiously.

"About what you know. This town. Vegas."

Nicky drove. He drove like a bat out of the hot hell that Las Vegas in August would have been without air-conditioned hotels and an endless gridwork of power lines.

The Corvette's sleek fiberglass frame flattened to the road like a pale panther as the powerful motor stretched its automotive sinews.

There was only the dark of the road, a white dotted line into the distance, and the flat black shambles of the mountains ahead huddling against a sky nearly as opaque.

Nicky glanced to the passenger seat. The T-tops were off, and the wind ruffled their heads. Most dames hated open-top cars, he reflected, swaddling their hairdos in scarves; a few ran their fingers through their hair, leaned their heads back, closed their eyes, and let the wind kiss them senseless.

Van von Rhine did neither. She sat unruffled, the dashboard illumination frosting her wind-tremored hair with the faintest of auroras. She looked dead ahead into the featureless dark and said nothing.

That suited Nicky. His eyes slid back to the empty road and emptier distance beyond it; the needle slipped farther up the luminous dial. The Vette had been engineered to fly. No mere earthbound patrol car could catch it. None prowled this endless waste by night anyway.

Nicky's eyes caressed the chrome lighter knob; there was nothing so cheerful when you were alone in the dark as the ember at the end of your own cigarette. But he didn't smoke anymore, he told himself, and he was no longer alone — not in this headlong flight to solitude, not in his dreams of a hotel worth rebuilding.

He braked the Vette so suddenly that it performed a flashy TV-style about-face. Sand sprayed the windshield. The headlights drilled into an endless tunnel of desert scrub. He punched them off, along with the motor. Sound and motion had quelled to instant peace and quiet. The mountains hunkered at their back again and ahead, ahead . . . Nicky got out of the car and went around to open Van's door.

She wasn't afraid, he had to give her that.

"Where are we?" she asked in the polite, interested tones of a tourist.

"About halfway between the Spectre Range and Shadow Mountain, not far from Devil's Hole. Nowhere."

She turned to survey the bulky shapes looming against the sky behind them. "Can I see these mountains from my hotel window?"

He thought for a moment, figuring. "Yeah. Yeah — I guess you could."

"They look like misty pink marble in the daylight."

"Everything looks different at night. That's your first lesson about Vegas. It's a twenty-four hour state of mind, an all-day, all-night kind of place. But night's when it really sparkles. Look."

Nicky tented his fingers on her shoulders and delicately swiveled her to face the intended finale of the long, silent drive.

"Oh . . ." Her awed, indrawn breath was more reward

than any expression on her face, had there been light enough to see it. "Is that . . . the city?"

Nicky nodded in the dark, to himself, without answering.

You had to come way out here to see it — Las Vegas, queen of clubs, hearts, diamonds, and spades, all rolled into one. Now, by night, she displayed her diamonds — the tangled webs of quivering light that flashed far away on the desert.

Nicky leaned against the Vette's fender and began explaining. Or trying to.

"Have you ever flown from L.A. to Tucson? Naw, but I have. It's five hundred miles of flat nothin', night or day or anytime in between. At night it's black as the jack of spades. Just black — bottomless as the Grand Canyon.

"The plane's jets are droning, and the cabin is real eerie, and you're studying the ghost of yourself in the window . . . then, halfway between L.A. and Tucson, this exploding rose of light blossoms in the dark below you, like some mushroom cloud of life, not death. It's fairy dust and fever, every firecracker you ever dreamed of on the Fourth of July, every headlight that ever seemed to be hurtling right into you. It just . . . explodes."

Van shivered suddenly. Nicky took off his sport coat, carefully, because a wrong rustle might ruin everything, and draped it over her shoulders, his eyes still on the distant light show.

"That's the way you got to look at Vegas, see? At night, in the dark. Then you don't see all the noisy, gaudy stuff — the stuff that I kinda like anyway — the stuff that makes some people think she's a tramp. At night, she's a lady." He laughed, maybe at himself for trying to explain the inexplicable. "At night she rakes all of her ice out of the safe and shines!

"Anyhow, that's how I see it. I used to come out here when I came home from school, just a kid with a driver's license and a crazy idea. Sometimes I used to watch those lights until the damn dawn came up and scared them away. I knew what Vegas was, what my Family and some others helped to make it. Maybe Vegas is just a crass commercial city with no reason to exist except to fleece fools.

"But she still outshines them all. And that's what I want the hotel to be — one nice, clean, crystal-clear little lightbulb in all that wattage. Just one little new light in the dark. But classy, so it stands out."

Van turned to him, saying nothing. Nicky smoothed the jacket lapels over her shoulders, then turned and opened the car door. She reentered the car as matter-of-factly as she had exited it.

Nicky boosted himself into the driver's seat without bothering to open his door, like he did when he was sixteen. He switched on and revved the motor, burned the headlights back into the night, and aimed the Vette's long, low nose straight at the exploding star of light ahead.

He didn't speak all the way back, and neither did she.

The Fontana-to-be looked disappointingly low-wattage when it loomed in the windshield once again. Nicky swept the car under its unlit canopy and escorted Van inside.

Someone had left a few lobby lights on. Van paused while he reclaimed his jacket. Her expression was noncommittal; tired, maybe. Nicky knew in his sinking heart that he hadn't proved a thing — not in the dark of the Love Moat, not in the deepness of the desert night — except maybe his own vulnerability. Swear words tangoed at the edges of his mind.

"Hey, hey, hey! Nicky! Wait up."

Together they turned back to the doorway. A man

stubbier than a three-quarter-smoked cigar was bustling through the glass doors. He wore a Hawaiian shirt and an impatient look.

"Say, Nicky boy! Where you been lately? Your mama's been worried, she tells me on the long-distance phone."

"My mama's been used to me keeping my own hours for seven years now," Nicky retorted.

"So your uncle's been worried." The man scanned the deserted lobby with quick deprecatory glances. "Give me a break, kid; this place's got no more potential than your brother Ralph's got for keno. Is this all you've done so far? Nothin'? Jeez, what a dump."

"It's in the planning stages."

"Planning, schmanning. Kid, forget this hotel. That's a lot of moola to throw down a rathole. Come back to the Family business where you belong. You don't stand a chance."

"This is not a rathole, Mr. Fontana."

Nicky stared. Van von Rhine hadn't spoken for so long that he'd forgotten that she could. His uncle Mario stared, too. He wasn't used to being contradicted by women.

"Of course," she went on in a dispassionate tone, "it takes a certain amount of capital to renovate a hotel into a first-class establishment. But the work itself should progress quickly once it's begun."

Uncle Mario's cigar-brown eyes jabbed Nicky's way. "Who's this mouthy broad?"

Nicky confined his smile to the corners of his mouth. "That's no broad, Uncle Mario. That's my new hotel manager."

Hairy hands fisted on hips decked in dazzling magenta and turquoise. "Oh, yeah? You and how many good fairies? This old dump's a DOA. That's 'dead on arrival,' sweetheart! No little Miss Prissy's gonna pull Nicky's fat outa the fire this time, not on a jinxed joint like this."

A subtle shuffle ground underfoot as Van von Rhine's cobalt silk pumps shifted to a wider stance. Her hands moved deliberately to her hips and her head tilted, jutting a porcelain chin delicately forward. Nicky edged back, not sure what from, except maybe a form of fireworks he'd never witnessed before.

" 'Oh, ye of little faith . . .' " she quoted for openers. "I don't see how a prominent person such as yourself, Mr. Mario Fontana, got anywhere at all in this cold, cruel world with that defeatist attitude!"

She advanced a step, her eyes flinging bolts of blue lightning. Mario Fontana stepped back before he could catch himself.

"I'll have you know that this 'old dump' is a perfect candidate for a stunning revival. It could become the finest and flashiest hotel Las Vegas saw on its better days. And it won't be done in cheap 'Miami Moroccan' or 'Hollywood Orgasmic' or 'Roman Orgiastic' or 'Organic Behind' style like the rest of the . . . the 'joints' in this town. Wait until you see it, Mr. Fontana," she almost threatened. One elegant hand-wave indicated the indifferent ceiling above them.

"Enough fountains, mirrors, and crystal to blind the telescope on Mount Palomar." Her wrist circled eloquently toward the dreary stretches of encircling wall. "A glass-enclosed circular pavilion with a running-water roof and a chain of lagoons, cocktail lounges, restaurants, carp pools, bridges, and whirlpools. Perhaps even a small waterfall. I'm undecided yet.

"And right where you are standing, Mr. Fontana, the very spot —"

Mario Fontana leaped back as if he had just sighted a

sheepdog-size cockroach. Van von Rhine's slender fore-finger pointed dramatically to the rumpled carpet at his feet.

"Right there will rise a Plexiglas column bearing a custom-commissioned Lalique crystal artwork in a form to mirror the hotel's new name — the Crystal Phoenix.

"The Phoenix, in case your study of the classics was interrupted by business concerns, Mr. Fontana, is a mythical bird that rose again from the ashes of its own body. *This* Crystal Phoenix will be the epitome of the architectural art as it is practiced in this rather tawdry town of yours. It will be the eighth wonder of modern Las Vegas."

Van von Rhine folded her arms and glared icily at Nicky's uncle Mario, who turned hastily to his nephew.

"Sounds . . . uh, good, Nicky. Smart thinkin'. Sure, I was just sayin', why not give the idea a try? Say, uh, it's late. I just stopped by to schmooze a little. Me and a few of the boys plan a little dawn-to-dusk poker match at the Dunes. So I'll say . . . *ciao*, Nicky. And, uh —"

He stared at Van, then turned in a blur of shirt as lurid as a Hawaiian sunset and vanished back into the midnight-black limo purring at the curb like a hungry panther.

Nicky looked around the lobby and along the length of muted slot machines and idle, blanketed crap tables. He looked up to the pedestrian ceiling, down to the litter-carpeted floor. He looked last at Van, and then, like the city he loved, he exploded into high voltage excitement.

"Ya-*hoo!*" An unpremeditated bear hug spun Van into his arms, around and around on the exact future spot of the Lalique column with the crystal phoenix. "Lady, you are on a roll tonight! Uncle Mario, uncle Mario . . . was speechless! What an act; what a bluff! Yahoo!"

A royal-blue sandal went spinning across the rug, then

another. Nicky turned exuberantly until he was dizzy and breathless from laughing. Odd thing, he noticed. Van von Rhine was laughing, too.

"Nobody, but nobody, faces off uncle Mario!" he chortled. "Not even Ugly Al Fresco. You better watch it, baby, or he'll be mixing his concrete booties in a size six."

"No, he won't." She was eyeing him shrewdly as he stopped and diffidently lowered her back to the floor.

Van von Rhine was not the pickupable type, Nicky remembered tardily. But only the tips of her stockinged feet touched earth yet, and her well-packaged weight hung pleasantly from his shoulders. "You're his favorite nephew," she pointed out.

"So I am. Or was. I love it! 'This is no broad, this is my new hotel manager. . . .'" Nicky laughed convulsively, his deep breaths inadvertently drawing her lily-of-the-valley scent into his pores, the satin of her hair against his cheek. He let her go as soon as he perceived it, quickly.

"What a great con," he said, going to retrieve her far-flung shoes.

She waited, calm as a barefoot princess in her throne room, for his return. Nicky found himself kneeling to offer first one satin slipper, then the other, while her fingers pressed his shoulder for balance and her small foot arched neatly into his hand.

He'd been right from the first; she had world-class legs. Nicky's eyes followed his own conclusion up a well-turned length of ankle, calf, and knee to thigh. . . . He stood abruptly.

"So. When did you dream up this face-saving fairy tale? On your feet? While uncle Mario was trying to put my . . . uh, behind . . . in a Philistine sling?"

Her eyes were grave, as crystalline blue as Lake Mead. A

guy could drown in such lucidity, Nicky thought in confusion, trying to name it. Maybe it was honesty.

"It . . . came to me in the car, on the way back," she was saying, almost shyly. "I started thinking about everything I've seen here and what the hotel could be. Your uncle Mario simply forced me to say what I'd already decided."

"You mean all that's for real? The water, the crystal, the, the . . . imitation Love Moat?"

"For real. Only better. And not an imitation, the real thing. You'll see when I get an architect to draw up some plans. Your hotel will shine, Nicky, I promise."

Her eyes mirrored her promise, mirrored other things, maybe, that Nicky didn't want to lean too close and accidentally spot. It wasn't polite to look at someone's cards when you were just kibbitzing, not really playing the game for keeps. He rubbed a nervous hand over the back of his neck and patted the pocket where his cigarette case reposed without being aware of the gesture.

"Ah, it sounded great. You've sold me, but —"

"I'm sorry about the name," she said quietly. "It's just that the Crystal Phoenix will be much more marketable. More in keeping with Las Vegas . . . glitz, if you know what I mean. It has ooomph." Her hand wobbled in a way that Nicky recognized from some place far away and long ago.

He took a stabilizing stroll around the empty lobby, while ego of ownership suffered a decent interment in his mind.

"Okay," he concluded. "I guess that's what I wanted — for you to see what this hotel could become, for you to grab onto a piece of my dream."

He looked at her again. She was shining. She knew what she was doing finally, and why. She cared. She gave a damn. His hotel was her hotel. It was a scary thought.

"Let's . . . let's get upstairs to bed," he said, wanting privacy. Instantly, he cursed the unfortunate implication of his casual words, even in a hotel of many beds.

Van had already turned for the elevators, apparently having thought nothing of it. Nicky felt vaguely insulted and definitely relieved.

He saw her to her room by the weak light of a single wall sconce, but stopped her fingers as they turned the knob.

"About tonight," he said. "In the" — he laughed nervously — "the Love Moat. I'm sorry. That's not my style. I was just so damn exasperated."

She looked at him limpidly, every hair in place, her voice level, her eyes unblinking. "What is your style?"

"I don't know," Nicky said, rummaging for the words that usually came so glibly. "I don't know." He tilted her chin to the light, to his face, and gently brushed her mouth with uncertain, apologetic lips.

In the elevator Nicky breathed a free man for the first time that evening. Goodbye, Fontana; hello Crystal Phoenix. The Crystal Phoenix. Nicky's eyes narrowed as he pictured a scintillating marquee in electric-blue neon. The doll was right; the name had oomph.

It had a definite ring to it. He grinned and hooked his jacket over his shoulder. Maybe they could put "Fontana" on a lounge at the top. . . .

♣ Chapter Nine ♣

MIDNIGHT LOUIE REFLECTS ON BENCHMARK EVENTS

So this is the first time I hear the name, the night Macho Mario Fontana gets read the riot act by this little doll in stiletto heels and what you might call dudgeon almost as high.

The Crystal Phoenix, she says, like she has it tucked in the back of her mind all along. The name tickles my fancy even then, the first time I hear it, and I am getting to an age when not much tickles my fancy, not to mention other unmentionable things.

Naturally I am there on the scene, although the Crystal Phoenix is just a light bulb in the brain of a feisty little doll at the time and I am not yet prevailed upon to take an official role in the establishment.

My usual modest profile keeps the principals in this little drama from observing my presence, which is just as well, as nobody acts with characteristic grace that night.

Of course I keep my lips zipped about the incident. Macho Mario is known for fancying filet of snitch, a dish of which he and his entire Family are most fond. And Mr. Nicky Fontana, well, he is a prince, but even princes do not take to being outflanked by feisty dolls with cute little French rolls on their heads . . . or any witnesses thereto.

So I keep my usual low profile, but already I scent some opportunity on the premises for a freelance fellow-about-town like myself. I resolve to hang around and see what I can turn up. For one thing, I have a way with women, if I do put forth that opinion myself, and it is clear that Mr. Nicky Fontana can benefit from a more seasoned example on that score.

And that little hotel doll does not scare me one iota. Indeed, I expect to have Miss Van von Rhine eating out of my mitt within the fortnight — or vice versa — or my name is not Midnight Louie and the Crystal Phoenix is not about to become the classiest flophouse in Vegas.

♣ Chapter Ten ♣

Van stood marooned in the deserted lobby, her arms cradling rolls of architectural plans. Her high heels almost precisely marked the spot she had assigned the evening before to a not-yet-existent plinth of Plexiglas upholding a rare crystal mythological bird.

She turned slowly, mimicking the wild carousel motion of Nicky's impulsive embrace, which also seemed a mere figment of the previous night's excesses. Today, Van saw only cold daylight reality extending in all directions.

She must have been mad! Or perhaps she simply had been angry — angry to see uncle Mario in the lurid flesh laying a wet Fontana Family blanket all over Nicky's fragile aspirations. Now her shoulders tautened as she contemplated the work needed to realize the bravado of her midnight vision. Even Erick von Rhine might have quailed at the task.

Far down the hall, a slight, anonymous figure moved from one wall to the other. Van observed it indifferently, lost in contemplating the gargantuan task of transforming the Joshua Tree into the Crystal Phoenix. She felt like a David handed a paper sling.

"Hi! Is Nicky up?" a breezy female voice called.

Startled, Van could only blurt "I don't know" at the lithe, long-legged young woman who had materialized before her, a fuchsia canvas gym bag butting softly against her slender shins.

The young woman grinned. "I know what you mean. Listen, I hate to barge in this early, knowing what hours he keeps, but my pulled calf muscle desperately needs that rooftop whirlpool of his. I'm Darcy McGill and I wouldn't be butting in on your territory, would I?"

"Me? Certainly not," Van sputtered, juggling rolls of plans like loaves of French bread. "I have nothing to do with the man," she insisted emphatically if not quite accurately.

"That's what they all say," Darcy commented, laughing. She extended a slim, strong hand for a businesslike shake. "I'll just run up and rattle Nicky's cage, then. See you around later, whoever you are."

She was gone, sprinting for the elevator with agile grace despite the supposed muscle injury. Van sourly watched the silver doors of the penthouse elevator swallow her shorts-clad figure. Obviously, Van could expect small help from Nicky's quarter as long as he kept the chorus line coming and going, in eager rotation.

"Here, Miss von Rhine, let me help you with those."

Van turned to find a beaming Walter Maxwell, his balding head dewed by early-morning Las Vegas humidity. How people managed to slip in and out of the hotel so cavalierly Van couldn't imagine, but she gratefully transferred a third of the slipping rolls to his waiting arms.

"At last a logical mind! Where, Mr. Maxwell, can I find the erstwhile manager's office?"

"This way." Maxwell scuttled eagerly in the direction indicated, glancing back at her armful of plans. "Your additional luggage arrived safely, I see."

"So to speak, if anything can be said to be 'safe' in Las Vegas." Van marched grimly alongside the little man. "Including one's sanity."

Maxwell let that comment slide into home plate unheralded. "And how are the renovation plans proceeding?"

"Peachy!" Van snapped.

He stopped, forcing Van to pause. "It's Nicky, isn't it? He's not taking this project seriously —"

"Oh, he's taking the *project* seriously." Van's voice softened as she recalled the distant city lights shimmering at full power against the velvet-painting backdrop of a desert night, and remembered being whirled into conspiracy with Nicky's effusive dreams in this very lobby. Whirled. Whirlpool. Girlpool. She spoke sharply.

"But there doesn't seem to be any likelihood of Mr. Fontana's putting in the sustained time and sheer blood, sweat, and tears required."

Maxwell nodded sympathetically. "That's why this hotel could be so good for him. Nobody ever expected much of Nicky, least of all the Family, except gratitude while they handed him everything on a platter."

"I'm here to renovate a hotel, not rehabilitate a . . . a playboy who lives in a penthouse," Van fumed, preceding the lawyer through an unlabeled door, past several vacant desks, and into an office marked "Manager."

"Do you think it's possible?"

"With Nicky Fontana, everything is *im*possible!"

"I meant revamping the hotel," Maxwell put in meekly.

"Oh, that . . . Well —" Van perched on the Goliath-sized tufted leather managerial chair behind the desk and tilted unexpectedly backwards. She stood. "Oh, get me a good secretarial chair from the reception desk, please; these overstuffed, oversprung status symbols are worthless for *working* managers!"

Maxwell hurriedly skated a chair from the next room into place while Van herded the leather behemoth away from the huge desk.

"Seriously," he asked, "how does the project look?"

"Like a lot of work and a lot of money." Van thoughtfully

unrolled the plans, using abandoned Coke bottles to pin down their curling edges.

"Sounds like a job for Superman," suggested a new voice. They looked up to see a smiling Nicky Fontana holding up the door frame with outstretched arms, and attired in yet another silk shirt and semi-knotted tie. "I woke up early, so I thought I'd see what's cooking. Hi, Maxie, you seen anybody I should know lately?"

"Only Nostradamus, planning to pay you off on a bet."

Nicky laughed and went to sprawl in Van's rejected chair, looking like he belonged there.

"I thought you had company," Van remarked shortly, still shuffling papers.

"Unexpected company," Nicky emphasized. "Maxie, see if you can talk Nostrodamus out of my money; I've got a feeling rhymin' Simon will be heard of but not seen around here, now that he owes *me* dough for a change."

"Sure," Maxwell said, rising. He was lawyer enough to recognize a client's dismissal. "Take it easy," he adjured the room, carefully aiming his comment somewhere between its two occupants. Then he was gone.

"Whatcha doing?" Nicky inquired disingenuously, approaching the desk.

"Working."

"Uh-oh. You must have got up on the wrong side of a prickly pear this morning. What're you working *on,* then?"

"The hotel."

"Are all those plans for this joint?"

"Every last floor and broom closet. I'm trying to adapt my . . . our . . . far-fetched redesign scheme to reality."

"Hey, those are my digs, aren't they?" Nicky prowled on silent Gucci loafers behind Van's desk to study the drawings from the proper angle.

His hand braced itself on the low back of her chair, the knuckles pressing softly into her shoulder blade. Van stiffened, then swiftly reshuffled papers until the lobby floor plan rested on top.

"This is the key piece," she explained. "Once we establish the hotel's new theme in the marquee outside and carry it through the lobby, casino, and restaurant areas, redecorating the guest rooms should be a snap."

"I'm redoing the penthouse all by my lonesome, remember," Nicky warned. "Something in this place should be my private . . . preserve."

"I wouldn't have it any other way." Van turned to punctuate her remark's sincerity with a stern glance.

Nicky had leaned nearer to view the plans, his freshly shaven cheek pressing perilously close to hers, a tangy lime scent inundating her nostrils.

Van turned back to the desk. "We have to, of course, follow the rules of Las Vegas 'ambiance.' The nighttime exterior should outshine daylight, and the casino interior should resemble a night sky, dark and faintly twinkling."

"Where'd you get all that?" Nicky leaned so close to study the papers that the back support of Van's chair cracked in protest.

"Here." Van tapped a slim book while Nicky pronounced its lengthy title.

"*Learning from Las Vegas: The Forgotten Symbolism of Architectural Form*. You mean people write books about this town — *real* books, not just gambling guides?"

"Not 'people', a study group from the Yale University School of Art and Architecture."

"Well, I'll be damned! You mean I'm not crazy! This town is worth something? We *know* something here?"

"I mean that *some* well-educated people have found

method to its madness; all I have to do is decode it, and we'll have a hotel. Tom Wolfe called Las Vegas the Versailles of America, but then he's a journalist and prone to hyperbole."

"I don't care what this big, bad Wolf character — whoever he is — thinks, or what diseases he's prone to." Nicky's voice rumbled disconcertingly near Van's ear. "I just want to know if my hotel will be the tops? First-class?"

She kept her eyes unflinchingly forward. "First-class," she asserted. "If I find the time to do some preliminary groundwork."

"I get it." He straightened and withdrew.

Van's breath eased out with every step away he took. At the door he paused. Why not? Van thought fatalistically. The most effective torture was drawn out interminably.

"About . . . Darcy," Nicky said. "The lady upstairs." His dark head jerked upward toward the penthouse. "She's a . . . friend of mine, that's all. She needed a favor."

"So do I. Peace and quiet." Van donned her most nannyish glare and was rewarded by a shrug of Nicky's silk-clad shoulders and a last lazy parting glance.

"Honestly!" Van sighed as she reclaimed the office as hers alone. Her private . . . preserve.

She moved the Yale book aside; it contained much good advice on the psychology of Las Vegas architecture. She wished it were as helpful on the psychology of certain Las Vegas citizens.

But perhaps Nicky Fontana's psychology was not the real issue. The man's mind was clearer than a crystal phoenix. Good-time Nicky. Fast cars and women and some dabbling in dreams on the side. Such predilections were common enough among spoiled sons of wealthy families, blue-blooded or cold-blooded or both. What Van found maddening was her sudden inability to deal with it.

He made her nervous, especially since last night, she admitted to herself. Since the . . . Love Moat. She cringed. It wasn't fair! He'd surprised her in the dark to make a point, but there she was, a nervous wreck every time he came near her.

Just as her resolve to get everything but work out of her mind hardened into something resembling uncle Mario's supposedly useful cement, a presence catapulted to her desktop.

Four fat black paws pinned the plans as effectively and much more decoratively than Coke bottles. A large, indolent-eyed feline face squinted shut for a predestined chin scratch, which assumption Van obliged by offering her curled fingernails for a rubbing post.

"You silly courtyard cat! How did you sneak inside the hotel? What a gold-digger! You're interrupting my work. Do you think you can slide through life on charm alone? And you act like you *own* the hotel."

Van scratched the cat's pleasure-flattened ears and leaned near to confide in them: "Have I got the soulmate for you!"

Within a week, blue-lined floor plans wallpapered the office's empty walls, and both the stray black cat and the White Sheep of the Fontana Family came and went at their separate but lordly leisure.

The cat confined itself to curling up at Van's feet, sitting on the precise document she most wished to peruse or hanging soulfully over her luncheon tray.

The man satisfied himself with popping in unexpectedly, lounging in the rejected desk chair, aiming unsmoked cigarettes at various targets on the wall-pinned floor plans and asking too many questions.

"Haven't you got anything else to do but watch me work?" Van asked irritably one afternoon when the air-conditioning groaned to repel a particularly suffocating wave of late summer heat.

Nicky's shrug revealed the gold charm at the open neck of his knit sports shirt — apparently he wore it incessantly, Van thought. His smile unveiled a string of white teeth that could have served as an advertisement for a Beverly Hills orthodontist.

"You don't look like you're working," he noted.

"This is when I work most, deciding the theme. Once the architects and construction bosses come in, it's literally out of our hands."

"That's why I'm here," Nicky said in an I-told-you-so tone, "to consult at this vital stage." He pinched a cigarette between his thumb and forefinger, then threw it at the wall opposite. "Almost got the bar carousel that time," he crowed, rising to retrieve his makeshift dart.

Van rolled her eyes, then paused as a young Song of indeterminate identity entered bearing a lacquered tray. He/she placed it atop the desk, managing to obscure Van's working papers as precisely as the black tomcat did when he decided to favor her desk with his reclining presence.

"What's this?" Luckily, Van's exasperation was untranslatable and the young Song didn't linger long enough to observe and convey the boss lady's annoyance back to the kitchen.

Nicky leaned over to inspect the steaming cup. "Egg drop soup, one of Sing's delicacies." He twisted his tan wrist, inspecting the Rolex watch circling it. "Three p.m. and Chef Song's way of telling you that you skipped lunch — again." Nicky elevated a stainless steel dome with a waiter-like flourish. "And with one you get enough egg rolls for two. Why don't you take a break?"

"Why don't you give me a break?" Van demanded, exasperated. "You know I can't get anything done with you hanging around!"

"What are you trying to get done?" Nicky sat back to sample an egg roll as Van capitulated and began sipping the soup.

"Right now I'm assigning functions and names to the various public areas. The greenhouse restaurant will be the Rainbow Oasis, for instance."

"Greenhouse. Isn't all that overhead desert sunlight pouring through the glass going to cost big bucks to cool?"

"That's the beauty of this new German roofing system that runs colored water between panes of glass, any shade you want, to reflect or absorb light as needed. And you can spotlight it at night too. Tailor-made for Las Vegas sparkle."

Nicky leaned forward, elbows atop her desk, to trace the first-floor outline with an impeccable fingernail. "I suppose you don't want to call this exterior waterway the Dove Moat — to go with the bird theme?"

"Certainly not!" Van set aside the empty soup cup and picked up an egg roll. "Something like the Crystal Promenade should do it. It'll be an informal area anyway, with cocktail service and walkways. And" — she watched him warily — "I've closely examined the square footage of the penthouse and adjoining roof."

"How closely?" Nicky's eyebrows raised in an expression that was kissing cousin to a smirk.

"Close enough to decide that — look, Nicky, where's this infamous whirlpool of yours located, exactly? It's not on the plan."

"I added it," he confessed, turning the paper around to

study the faint blue lines crisscrossing it before targeting a spot with his thumb. "Yeah, right here. Big enough to seat six, yet small enough for two, if you get what I mean."

Dark eyes smiled up with impish significance. Van got precisely what he meant but wasn't about to admit it.

"It really doesn't matter *what* size your spa is! The point is that the unused portion of the roof should be converted into a starlight whirlpool area for the guests — if you don't mind commercial considerations impinging on your 'private preserve.' "

"Object, hell! That's a great idea!" Nicky snapped erect, his eyes widening to visualize the possibilities.

"Sultry starlit nights on the roof," he intoned in a husky radio-smooth baritone, "a split of champagne, bubbles in the glass and the fiberglass, a discreet wash of piped-in music — the guests will love it! Who would have thought the great von Rhine would come up with a sybaritic stunt like that?"

Van glared, more disconcerted by his use of a classy word like "sybaritic" than his implication.

"What'll we call it?" Nicky mused. "Midnight at the Oasis? The Crystal Seraglio? The Phoenix Nest?"

"Don't be ridiculous! Where do you get all that nonsense?"

"I did go to college, you know. I learned a *little* something."

"Not so you could prove it," Van snapped. "We'll worry about names later. All I need now is your permission to appropriate the area."

"Hey . . ." Nicky rose to leave, but first he leaned over the desk and took Van's chin in the palm of his hand, as he had the first time they met. "You don't need my permission for anything, Van. You're the boss. You don't need anybody's permission. Remember that."

She blinked into his Coke-dark eyes as another name for the whirlpool deck popped into her dazed mind — the Velvet Maelstrom.

"And don't work too late," he admonished from the doorway. "You were in better shape when you were running me ragged all over town at all hours, von Rhine. You look terrible lately."

Van stared at the door after he had exited, then sighed and rotated her head on her neck. "Terrible." Did he think thinking was such easy work? Someone had to bury herself in this office behind these stacks of floor plans and tease the Crystal Phoenix into full-plumed shape. Did Nicky Fontana think hotels hatched ready-to-grow from eggs?

None of these questions had an answer, but before she dismissed them Van reached down, avoided the oversized sleeping hummock of fur at her feet and dredged up her purse.

The black crocodile-backed mirror she'd bought in Paris showed a tight circle of her own face lit by unflatteringly bright desert daylight. Fatigue had inlaid faint cobalt half-moons into the mother-of-pearl whiteness of her skin just below her eyes, which held a haunted look.

Nicky Fontana was right about one thing; she looked terrible — and what was worse, didn't care. Van slipped the mirror away and pushed aside the empty tray.

Once the major decisions were made, she could call in the experts, blend into the background and gratefully let Nicky's insatiable curiosity bedevil some tile layer or glass installer. His fascination with her — if that was what it was — couldn't . . . wouldn't . . . last, she told herself.

By the time Van rolled the plans away and returned to

her rooms, the sun had long since transferred its sunset coloration to the Strip's winking neon display of gold, rose, orange, and scarlet lights.

The thin Swiss watch on her wrist said 9 p.m. but the bedside alarm clock, which had a tendency to stop, announced an optimistic seven-ten.

Van switched on the TV wearing its black pillbox of a cable TV unit, nowadays a hotel room familiar almost as pervasive as the stray cat had become, and kicked off her shoes. Then the phone rang — the first time in days.

"Yes?"

"You sound worried. You must have been expecting me to call."

"Don't be ridiculous, Nicky. Is something wrong?"

"Yes. It's nine o'clock and you haven't eaten dinner yet. Why don't you meet me in the lobby and we'll grab something along the Strip?"

"I was planning a quiet night in —"

"I know. That's why I called. Incidentally, you shouldn't stay down in the office this late alone; there are some unsavory characters roaming around."

"I know. But I almost never run into you."

"Not bad. I see I'm in for a tongue-lashing. Meet you downstairs in ten minutes."

Van sighed as the dial tone growled soothingly into her ear. She looked terrible. Nicky had seen every decent dress she had packed. The Strip depressed her. She didn't know what was wrong with her but was certain that Nicky would tell her, given the opportunity.

Ten minutes later she emerged from her room, having paired her blue silk heels with a matching blouse and the white suit-skirt she had worn that day. A pair of midnight-blue sapphires winked at her earlobes, a gift from her father one Christmas too long ago to recall. Perhaps it had been in Venice or Monte. . . .

The lobby, still half-lit, was deserted. Van paced, expecting promptness as the least Nicky could do in making a pest of himself. Instead, the nameless cat greeted her, massaging her calves with luxuriantly furred sides, looping past her like a sidewinder snake.

"Left your office hidey-hole, did you?" Van bent to pat it, then froze in midstoop, her every sense alerted. Something was wrong, something about the lobby, and it was ordinarily so unremarkable that she hardly noticed it.

She looked around. For once, it was truly deserted, its ever-present peripheral denizens absent. Except . . . Van walked toward the rear hallway, aware of a subtle halo of unauthorized light leaking from somewhere.

Her heels moved from carpeting to institutional tile, ringing loud all at once. Behind her, the cat stalked on velvet paws.

Voices murmured from behind closed doors — one angry, another too soft, too strangely soft, to be heard. Van's heels tapped out a reckless faster beat.

The light came from the executive offices, from under the closed door that led to them, she realized, which she never bothered to shut or lock . . . because nobody ever came around the hotel, nobody that mattered, that needed to have anything hidden from him.

She slapped her evening purse under her arm as she tried the knob, expecting resistance for no reason.

The door sprang open, hurling her into the long passageway with it, casting her into its full light. The voices, from her office down the inner hall, stopped.

She kept her steps fast but deliberate. Her office itself came as an anti-climax. It looked as she had left it, an undecorated rectangle of wall-tacked plans. Four men stood in it now, making its managerial spaciousness seem suddenly cramped. Four men — three middle-aged men in dark sports clothes and Nicky Fontana.

"I'm sorry," Van blurted. "If I interrupted anything, that is . . . I'll wait in the lobby."

Nicky nodded curtly, his face tautened into a cartoon-sharp parody of itself, like Dick Tracy's in the funny papers when she was a little girl and her nanny bought the American Sunday papers for her amusement.

Van felt like a little girl again, a little girl barging past the wrong closed door in the hotel she called home. She couldn't wait to leave. And apparently Nicky Fontana couldn't wait to see her leave.

"Go on, then," he said harshly. "Get out of here."

She automatically planted her feet, as she had with Macho Mario Fontana, although she was unaware of the similarity of the pose. "It's my office," she began in a too-high voice.

"Van — leave!"

She stared at Nicky. And then she looked beyond him. Her carefully pinned up plans hung askew. Her desktop was even a worse mess than she had left it. Everything had . . . shifted.

One of the men had edged beyond her now, between her and the door.

"I'll see you in the lobby, then," she was saying, backing away from what she saw, from what she thought she saw. A secret meeting; men — mob types; Nicky, the hotel. Ugly questions with uglier answers lurked just around the corner. *Blood is thicker than water* . . . maybe even than mutual dreams. *Family is Family . . . and never the twain shall meet —*

The man behind her made himself into a door — a

closed door — and she stopped.

"Let her go," Nicky said, his voice low, angry, quietly desperate.

"Maybe this is a sign," the man behind her said. "Hotels are a dangerous business, Fontana, especially for parties who don't know what they're doin'."

Heavy hands dropped without warning to Van's shoulders. She stiffened without turning, recognizing that a reaction would only incite a greater one.

"Is that why you're here, to give me a few pointers?" Nicky demanded with reckless, attention-drawing tenacity. "Is that it?"

"Yeah, that's it." One man spoke, but it could have been any of them. They looked like the three little pigs, Van thought — beefy and possessed of a brutish shrewdness. "You got nerve, Nicky boy, askin' *us* what we're doin' here, like you own the place or sumthin'."

Thug Number One, the spokesman, jabbed Nicky in the chest, right below the small gold charm, which twinkled wickedly in response. Numbers Two and Three, including the man behind Van, moved like swift lethal machines to Nicky, their porkchop hands sliding ever so lightly down his silken arms, then tightening to restraints.

"No!" Van stepped toward the intruders.

"Little lady . . ." Number One warned her off, not bothering to break eye contact with Nicky but holding up a forbidding hand.

"Stay out of it," Nicky said between clenched teeth, with patented cheap detective nobility, not looking at her either. It infuriated Van, the way they all acted as if she were not there, and yet all seemed obsessed with her presence.

Number One did something with his other hand, hard and fast to Nicky's stomach. Van never saw the blow, only

Nicky sagging in the grasp of his jailors. The charm jiggled obscenely in the light of the overhead fluorescent.

Then Nicky was twisting like a fish on a line, flailing his own arms. Thugs scattered as they lost control. Blows landed, air was expelled in savage, muttered bursts from male throats. Van felt trapped inside the life-sized silver screen at the wrong kind of movie.

"Stop it!" she shouted, unable to follow the action, unable to believe her eyes. "Get out of here, or I'll . . . I'll —"

She ran for the door, jerked it open and yelled down the hall. "Chef Song, bring your meat cleaver — !"

Of course he didn't understand English and of course the kitchen was at the wrong side of the hotel, but the visitors didn't know that — yet.

A man behind her grabbed her arm. She stepped back into him and ground her stiletto heel onto his instep with all the passion of a Spanish dancer.

A curse turned into a sharp pained wail. Behind her a winded voice gathered to grunt out a warning.

"Maybe this'll give you the idea, Fontana! Get out of the hotel business. It ain't healthy."

Van turned to find Number One patting Nicky's cheek in a parody of sinister affection right out of *The Godfather*. And Nicky — there was fire in his eyes, but two thugs secured his arms and blood blurred the edges of his face.

The men brushed past her on their way out, Number One pausing to address her as he left.

"Maybe you should get yourself a new boyfriend, girlie. This one's got no brains and less class, not to mention life expectancy."

He was gone. Van turned back into the room to find Nicky watching the door like someone on a leash. His eyes lowered as she stared and he turned to sit on the desk, using the discarded napkin on Chef Song's luncheon tray to dab at his cuts. White linen, Van's managerial brain noted dispassionately; blood would never wash out.

"Are you hurt?" She edged sideways into the room, her purse clasped before her, her back to the wall as if she expected bogeymen to leap out from everywhere. "What was that all about?"

"God knows," he said, then laughed. "Beating the kid to a pulp if you hadn't happened in, I guess. I heard something while I was waiting for you. When I came down the hall, I ran into the Three Stooges ransacking the office." He glanced up, looking like a real prizefighter this time. "Trust dames to be late and get a guy in trouble."

"I wasn't late!" Van was angry, she didn't know quite why or at whom. "And they wouldn't have been here at all if you hadn't had this crazy idea about a hotel — or if your uncle Mario hadn't been in the Family business up to his Havana cigars! And I wouldn't have been here, either, if you hadn't had your heart set on bringing 'class' to a city that wouldn't recognize the meaning of the word if it was spelled out in neon twenty stories high!"

"Hey —" Nicky was coming toward her, an expression on his battered face as if it were Van who had been attacked and needed soothing.

"Stay away from me!" The wall was at her back now, and she edged even farther along it until she felt the right-angle reassurance of a corner. "Stay away! I don't want to see you, I don't want to know about things like this. It's crazy, Nicky, you can't do anything good in a rotten town like this! I should never have come. I wouldn't have, except . . . except —"

"It's nothing. I'm fine. Those bozos couldn't dust off a fruit fly. My brothers did worse when I was nine."

Nicky had boxed her into the corner and Van didn't know where to look so that she wouldn't see his worried face coming at her wearing an expression of cautious solicitude, as if *she'd* been hurt when any fool except Nicky Fontana could see that it was he who needed help.

"Let go of me!" Van ordered in her best uncle-Mario-banishing voice as his hands clasped her arms.

Nicky's face came closer, the blood already drying on his cheek, the bruises already setting alongside the cuts like small swollen purple suns.

"No," he said softly, as dangerously determined as any gangster. "No."

♣ Chapter Eleven ♣

MIDNIGHT LOUIE REGISTERS A GRIEVANCE

I am used to being overlooked, as I have said before, and I do not really expect a guy and doll who just repelled three of the more repellent extant examples of Las Vegas muscle to pay much attention to me.

My feelings are somewhat hurt that they express no concern for my welfare, but then I am in my retreat at the darkest corner of the lobby, and I am discreet normally, so when I am trying to be subtle, I am almost invisible. Besides, I have no wish to attract the attention of the three refugees from Muscle Beach should they decide they have forgotten to attend to some little thing — such as myself — and return.

I am entering what the sociologists like to term the golden years and am in no shape to defend myself, much less anyone else, though I will always holler for help for a friend.

So my not inconsiderable person is successfully camouflaged between a pillar and a potted palm of my acquaintance that in its salad days was a fine specimen but now is somewhat dead, and neither Mr. Nicky Fontana nor the little doll see me when he escorts her back to the lobby.

Well, needless to say, the thought of dinner does not sit so good on anyone's stomach, including mine — although I am not averse to slipping by Dome of the Sea for a small snack later.

Miss Van von Rhine is one subdued doll as Mr. Nicky Fontana leads her to the elevator, and I can discern, even from the dark, that she is upset more than somewhat.

But Mr. Nicky Fontana is a prince, as I indicated before, and he just guides her along with his arm around her shoulders, whispering whatever guys whisper to more than somewhat upset little dolls.

I have never seen so spirited a lady undergo such a change of temperament in my whole lengthy lifetime, which is as long as a high-roller's credit, and I am not optimistic about Mr. Nicky Fontana's being able to bring this little doll around, not with his personal performance record with same little doll.

It is a long, dark, lonely night, and I am not optimistic about anything, I decide.

♣ Chapter Twelve ♣

"This is *your* floor!"

"They're *all* my floors." Nicky grinned into Van's wide, Lake-Mead-blue eyes as he escorted her along the corridor to the penthouse door. "At least you're noticing where you are now."

"Yes," she agreed with a start, her shoulder shrugging off his custodial arm. Nicky stiffened at the rejection, then relaxed and elaborately backed away before speaking.

"I, for one, plan to clean up before I decide if I still want to go out for dinner." He winced while massaging his stomach with his palm. "That guy's fist was packing a roll of quarters, or I'm an anteater."

"Oh." Van trailed him into the darkened penthouse, as if realizing just then that Nicky's wounds were more than a Technicolor effect on a distant screen. "Does it . . . hurt?"

He turned on the overhead track lighting and faced her with another deprecatory grimace. "Yeah. 'More than somewhat,' to quote some literary gent, now dead."

She smiled. " ' 'Tis not so deep as a well, nor so wide as a church-door, but 'tis enough, 'twill serve,' " Van quoted back.

"Who's *your* literary gent?"

"William Shakespeare, now dead, too."

"Oh, yeah, him. I guess literary gents don't last long. What play was that from, anyway?"

Van cleared her throat. "Romeo and Juliet."

Nicky stared at her. "Yeah . . . right." He turned and lurched down the hallway.

Van waited. Under the bright penthouse lighting, it was impossible to fool herself that Nicky's wounds, that the entire ugly scene in her office, weren't real. Nicky looked as if he'd been run through a wringer backward, despite his glib jokes. He looked, in short, awful.

Van set down her evening bag with sudden resolution and moved purposefully down the hall after him.

She found Nicky bracing himself on a black porcelain pedestal sink itself supported by a column upheld by three more than somewhat coy cherubs. He was dabbing at his facial cuts with a black washcloth, in the process sprinkling more water on his silk shirt than on his wounds.

"This is atrocious decor." Van glanced grimly around the halfbath, appropriating the washcloth.

Nicky made no protest but sat against the sink edge and studied the room while Van rubbed his already tender face with stringent German efficiency and some alcohol she'd found in the medicine cabinet.

"What's wrong with this decor?" he asked sharply, more a measure of physical discomfort than hurt sensibilities.

"It's cheap . . . tawdry," Van retorted, slathering on alcohol despite his winces. "Black, white, and gold went out as a bathroom color scheme with Attila the Hun. The orgy wallpaper is gauche, the filigree lighting fixture belongs in a brothel, as does most of what passes for decor in this town, and the tap handles don't turn easily."

She savagely tweaked the gilt tails of brass peacocks posing as sink hardware and released a stream of rapidly overheating water.

"Take it easy, lady," Nicky pled only half jokingly. "First you try to scrub me to death. Now you're trying to boil my backside!"

He jumped away from spattering hot water and began

unbuttoning his now fully sodden shirt.

Van turned to shut off the water.

"Thank you, Miss Vanessa."

She whirled to face him. "Why do you call me that?"

He shrugged, plastering the wet silk more tightly to his torso. "Van . . . Vanessa. Makes sense. And a Vanessa would be an efficient, well-controlled female, a cool hand in an emergency, organized to the point of folding a wet washcloth into fours and putting it neatly away —"

Van jumped guiltily and hurled away the washcloth her hands had been absently quartering in just the manner he described. It hit the ebony sink side with a plop and ad- hered in a satisfactorily messy lump. The action did not deter Nicky, who was busy peeling himself out of his shirt.

Van found the process prolonged and rather suggestive. She concentrated instead on the curious medallion at his throat.

"You're lucky those men didn't walk off with that. It must be worth something."

Nicky clasped the small medal in a protective fist as if just remembering it. "It's worth something to me."

"What is it?"

He paused in disrobing, looking first sheepish, then cun- ning. "If I tell you, will you tell me?"

"No baptismal names."

"Then promise not to laugh?"

"I never laugh, remember? No sense of humor."

"If I tell you, will you tell me why that scene downstairs tore you up so much?"

"I don't know," Van said. "I really don't know."

He looked at her for a long time, then released the charm as if it no longer needed guarding. It fell against his bare chest, bright as a coin spinning on a rich walnut tabletop.

"St. Jude," Nicky confessed. "It's a medal of St. Jude. The Saint of the Impossible."

Van had nothing to say in the face of this childish and somehow touching faith, except finally to smile. "I always said you were impossible."

"You don't know the half of it," he began, edging nearer.

She eluded him by going to examine the clear vinyl shower curtain with its drawings of Greek gods and goddesses in imaginatively compromising positions.

"I didn't put this stuff in, for God's sake!" Nicky exploded. "I just live here, remember?"

"What are you going to do now?"

Nicky shrugged. "I don't know. Hit the jets, I guess, before I stiffen like a corpse. Those guys and me, we tussled more than it looked."

He left the room and Van followed. " 'Jets'?" she asked uncertainly.

He grinned at her over his shoulder, one eye already swelling slightly shut. He would look hideous by morning. "Jets. Come on. You can view the infamous whirlpool."

En route, he paused at the mirrored bar, regarded his battered face, winced, and poured three fingers of brandy into a snifter. He handed that glass to Van and poured six fingers into another.

"Without dinner?" Van inquired sharply.

"Lady, it's my stomach, and right now it needs anesthetic."

Pushing aside the sliding glass door, Nicky ushered Van onto the open rooftop. The heat felt unexpectedly heavy after the icy interior air-conditioning.

Unlucky or not, the thirteenth floor loomed high enough above a mostly low-profile city so that Van and Nicky seemed alone with the darkness. Above them, the night sky swung open its robes to reveal a black velvet lining stitched with stars. Van roamed the redwood deck, studying flowering bushes in their pots, looking to the vastness of the black horizon, empty of skyscrapers except for the distant lighted towers of the major Strip hotels.

"Any complaints about the decor?" Nicky was swirling the brandy in his glass. He brought it to his lips, paused, and then sipped, his expression hamstrung between pleasure and pain.

"None," Van said simply. She carefully minced her needle-narrow heels around the cracks between the redwood planks leading to some risers. At the top of the steps, under a latticework gazebo trellised by climbing roses pregnant with full-blown scent, the inset whirlpool foamed furiously.

"I fail to see the attraction."

If her comment reminded Nicky of another unfortunate evening near an artificial body of water, his face didn't show it.

"It's not so bad; soothes the savaged soul." He came over to take her brandy snifter and set it down with his on a bench. "You should try it. Your muscles'll feel like they lifted weights in the morning. You were pretty uptight down there."

"I don't ordinarily encounter thugs in the process of accosting my acquaintances!" Van turned away, as if the sight of Nicky Now reminded her too painfully of Nicky Then. "What did those men want? And why? And what will you do about it?"

"I'll worry about that later. Now I need some tender loving hot water."

Van froze as a belt buckle clinked behind her, followed by the grate of a zipper.

"Come on," Nicky urged, "hop in. There are some extra bikinis around if you're shy."

"There *would* be!" Van exploded, so outraged that she whirled to face him.

Horrified, she let her glance drop to check what she should have ascertained before turning — his dark Jockeys were no more modest than European-style swimtrunks, which was not saying much for their efficiency.

But Nicky's attention was totally focused on her now. Barefoot, he was unnervingly even with her high-heeled height.

His face seemed conspiratorially near as he crooned, "Relax, Van. It's over. Things like that happen all the time in Vegas. I know how to deal with it, but I don't think you do. Just get loose and let go a little . . ."

He reached for her, and she backed away, jamming a heel in a crack.

"My silk blouse — you'll get it wet! Oh, fudge! My shoe!"

He knelt to work her foot loose, finally pulling her instep free while he twisted out the recalcitrant heel. One-footed, Van was forced to balance herself with one hand on Nicky's bare shoulder and recall a similar, more emotional scene the night before.

The whirlpool was veiling them with a warm invisible mist, and the subtle play of the muscles under Van's fingers sent shivers up her arm and down her spine. How, she wondered, had she gotten herself into this ridiculous position? She should know better than to come to hotel roofs, after the unsettling incident in Munich. . . .

"Free at last!" Nicky flourished the liberated sandal between them as he rose. "Better ditch the other one."

While Van again stooped to use him for a hand rest,

Nicky claimed the second shoe. When he had the pair, he tossed them aside, bent, and slipped an arm under Van's knees.

"Nicky, what are you doing?" She was screeching like a teenager, which only made him chuckle as he lifted her.

In three quick descending steps he was in the whirlpool, sinking into the fevered water with Van in his arms. She was screaming in full voice now, her fists clenched clichés beating at his arms and chest.

"Stop it! You . . . you thug! You unmitigated *savage!* I'm getting all wet . . . My silk blouse — Nicky, you're impossible, and you're drowning me! Oh, my *beautiful* blue blouse. . . ."

She rose from the bubbling water like a vengeful dryad as Nicky reclined on his underwater bench, arms wide along the spa's curved fiberglass sides, and surveyed his handiwork.

"See, it's not so bad. Kind of relaxing, actually."

"Relaxing! You're a Vandal! A Hun! You've ruined my clothes . . . even my hair's soaking! Hasn't anybody ever taught you any manners?"

"Hasn't anybody ever taught you anything else?" he retorted, suddenly leaning inward.

His hands kept her from thrashing in the water that roiled around her hips. They were suddenly close to each other, the night was their private spangled black beach umbrella, and thugs existed only as a preface to a much longer and more involved story.

Nicky's fingers rose from the foaming water to tease the silk-covered top button of her blouse. "It's ruined already. Why not get rid of it?"

His voice had gone low, and the intensity of his eyes deepened as his face drifted nearer to Van's, his cut lips moving toward hers.

"You're — depraved," Van breathed without conviction.

Nicky's hands relentlessly descended the seam of her wet blouse, rending loose one button after the other. They were everywhere, underwater, easing the silky lingerie straps off her shoulders, at her French twist, pulling hidden pins loose and letting damp waves of hair brush her water-misted shoulders.

By the time their lips met, Van was conscious only of floating in a benign, bubbling environment while pieces of her everyday skin flayed away into the midnight distance. All she could hear was the soft, persuasive rise and fall of the voice so near her ear, it seemed an echo of her own thoughts. All she could feel was how divinely right this moment, these sensations, felt. Van could no longer tell which sensation was her own and which was his as they rocked together in the lulling water.

Finally Van broke away and heaved herself back in the water to look at him. Mercurial Nicky at last was still, statue still, looking back at her. Laughter and lust had vanished like bubbles. Only the jet-propelled water moved, restless and caressing.

He sat back in the whirlpool, opposite her, and they viewed each other across the small expanse of foaming water, as fighters do, used to marking their encounters in the measured cadence of rounds.

"You look like a Southern Belle," Nicky said suddenly, with a smile.

Van glanced down. A ruffle of white bubbles unfurled around her bare shoulders. He turned away, reaching for the brandy snifter. Van caught her breath. Nicky turned back and stretched out an arm in mute invitation. She could have lunged full length in the water, kept herself half-hidden.

Instead, she stood, slowly, shyly, the warm water curdling away from her body like a second skin.

"Now you look like a Vegas show girl," he said. "No. Classier. Like that Venus that's all hair and skin in that famous painting by . . . by Vermicelli."

"Botticelli," she corrected indulgently.

"Whatever. Us Italian guys sure can paint." His outstretched hand reached for her. "We can do other stuff, too."

He laughed suddenly and pulled her down beside him, into the crook of his arm, offering her mouth the lip of the brandy snifter instead of his, as she had expected.

"Clear your senses; it kind of unnerves me to see a classy lady looking like she's thinking of doing a strip-tease."

"How could I be? I don't have anything left on to tease you with."

"Want to bet?" Nicky asked tenderly, tilting the brandy to her lips then setting the goblet quickly aside and kissing her as if to share the heady sizzle of the taste.

Nicky was a verbal lover; he vocalized uninhibitedly, purring and chirping and growling.

"Oh, Vanessa mine, you are not only efficient by day but a tigress by night," he was teasing.

Van's hands hit the water flat, sending up a plume of spray. "I'm *not* a Vanessa! Why can't you just call me Van, like everybody else?"

"It's not very romantic, love," Nicky answered, doing something not very romantic but most effective to the back of her knees. "And I'm not 'everybody else,'" he added, proving that by kissing her until their mouths seemed to merge in sheer osculatory oblivion.

"Now was that first class or not?" he demanded on parting.

"I don't know how you can —" Van, serious again, was appalled by how natural it felt to be cavorting in a whirlpool with a man she hardly knew in any real sense.

"How I can what?"

"Laugh off things, like earlier tonight . . . and now."

His thumbs stroked soothingly along her jawline and ended up massaging the tense muscles along the top of her shoulders.

"What's eating you, is it something you're afraid of?" His expression sharpened with an unwelcome thought, then turned solicitous. "Are you still a virgin?"

"No!" She had shouted the word from the rooftop almost before his last word emerged, so it was impossible to tell which question she denied so violently. "Does that take the fun out of it?"

"No. I just wonder what hurt you."

"You," she murmured. "You hurt me when you stop touching me and start talking. Kiss me again, Nicky, touch me. . . ."

It was too blatant an invitation to resist. Even though a frown had creased Nicky's forehead, it soon eased away. He was as lost as she. It was so surprising, this fevered love-making between two personalities seemingly as unmixable as oil and water.

To Nicky, it held a poignancy — a feeling as foreign to him as the word normally was. A preciousness. A magic. His mind searched for a way to name it, this surprising meeting between two creatures from vastly different worlds. He felt as if he'd picked up a porcupine and found a kitten.

She was murmuring feverishly now, too, all the right words, or rather, the right word over and over. "Yes," she was saying whenever their lips parted long enough for one or the other to get a word in edgewise, no matter how abbreviated. "Oh, yes, yes, yes. . . ."

Separation seemed an obscenity, but he stepped out of the still-churning water and made sure she didn't slip on the way out. Then they went barefoot and dripping through the ankle-deep shag of the living room and up the spiral staircase to the bedroom.

Nicky hit the light switch with a sure touch in the dark. Lights sprang into life all around them, but their eyes were already linked as if by something that didn't require illumination to connect perfectly.

Hers were a rich, limpid blue — how could he have looked at her so much and not noticed that until now? They were a blue deep enough to drown in, and that's what he was doing. He hardly saw the bed, only felt its broad liquid surface sink under him as they lay together upon it.

Her skin, untouched by the desert sun, seemed whiter than the Carrara marble statues outside Caesars Palace. He was beginning to fathom what "class" meant, and it wasn't the cold, distant thing he had thought it was. Nicky swallowed.

"You're sure?"

She nodded gravely, pale ripples of her hair dipping onto her shoulders. He wished he were that hair, that he could touch her with such exquisite lightness.

Some "literary gent" in his required freshman English Lit class had expressed the same idea three hundred years ago, he felt vaguely, but he had a bum mind for memorization — unless it was counting cards in a game of Twenty-one — and couldn't even fumble for the faraway words.

Instead he brushed back the hair from her temples and began encompassing her face with small, neat, endless kisses. Her fingers combed into his hair and pressed his lips closer.

"Nicky . . . you're so . . . sweet." She sounded surprised. He smiled through his kisses.

"Tell me afterward if you think I'm sweet," he advised, reaching into the bedside table for a contraceptive. It was a popular notion that Nicky Fontana was the quintessential eternal child, but he prided himself on being responsible when it counted. He came to her invited, drawn in.

When it had finally trembled to a stop and they lay in each other's arms, their faces buried — hers in his shoulder, his in her hair — as if to hide what was ordinarily most visible from this extraordinarily hidden intimacy, when it was over as any human act must be, they were silent.

Nicky pulled the covers over them, feeling a little like an Adam who had just been shown the flaming sword and the fast way out of Eden, with Eve to look after. Why he felt that way, he couldn't have said; Van would have bristled at the idea of being "looked after" by anyone, especially him of all people. Of all people.

He smiled his lazy post-coital satisfaction and fell soundly asleep. It was probably exactly what Adam had done, after the Fall.

♣ Chapter Thirteen ♣

"Rise and shine, Evangeline."

Van's upper lip twitched at the featherweight touch of a fingertip. Her eyes blinked open. Nicky's forefinger was rhythmically stroking her eyelashes upward.

"Why don't you use mascara?" he was asking in a lazy, besotted tone of voice. "Most blondes do."

"I don't know . . . You look awful!" she bluntly told him to his bruising face.

"It's a good thing I've been looking at you all night, then," he commented calmly.

She rolled her eyes heavenward, uncomfortable as the focus of such concentrated attention, and found slices of herself, and his self, reflected back. Surprise provided a pretext for pushing herself up against the headboard and away from Nicky's morning-after ardor.

"What is that?" she demanded. "Mirror strips inset between red velvet — *padded* red velvet?"

Nicky rolled onto his back to consider the upholstered ceiling: long slivers of mirror above and behind them reflected their bare anatomy. Tactful lengths of red velvet edited out the more inciting sections.

"I inherited it," Nicky said, disclaiming the decor, "like Mama Tinucci's money. It's not my fault. Round waterbeds normally aren't my style either."

"Round?" Van bobbed up in horror, clutching the sheet to her bosom just in time. The morning after rash sex, she couldn't help observing to herself, a breast invariably becomes a bosom. *Waterbed?*

Her fingers tightened on the sheet as her widening eyes began to apprehend the room's screamingly overblown decor. Her fingers tightened on the sheet . . . on the *red satin* sheet . . . then nearly loosened it, except that Van had decided that discretion was the better part of disgust.

"Nicky, that's gold-veined, antique-style mirror tile slathered all over this place!"

"You're right," he said consolingly. "Your eyes don't go with this decor. I'll change it. I was planning to anyway." He rolled over on the gelatinously shifting slick bedding. "None of this is the real me," he reassured her between kisses.

Van stared aghast at his face, now clearly wearing the badges of his assault. She was undecided whether to laugh or cry — or simply call for help.

"I can't believe I'm here," she finally managed to say.

"You can't believe which: that you made love in a room as lowbrow as this, or with me?"

"Neither. Both. I . . . don't know."

Nicky's forefinger pressed silence to her lips, his face straining upward to meet hers. Van found her chin dipping to accommodate him, her lips yearning toward his own, when the door thirty feet across the red shag carpeting cracked open.

"Anybody up? Oops! Sorry, Nicky, that's a bad joke. It's just Darcy. I needed the whirlpool again, and you said anytime . . . are you in there, Nicky? The penthouse door was unlocked."

He swore softly, then lifted his head to answer. "Yeah, I'm here. Go ahead and use the spa. I'll . . . uh . . . I won't be out before you leave."

"Roger, Nicky!" Darcy's blithe voice faded as she progressed back down the spiral staircase.

Nicky rolled off the bed and vanished around one of

many bloated swags of red velvet festooning it. Van looked warily around in his absence. She'd never seen a larger or more loathsome bedroom, not even in an Arab sheik's suite at the Athens hotel. Even a self-made Greek shipping tycoon would scorn such crass, barbaric splendor.

Nicky reappeared from around the bed curtains, white duck pants his only uniform of the morning. "Sorry we got pinned in here by Darcy —"

"How could you forget to lock the door after . . . after those men last night? We could have been killed in . . . in *your* bed."

Van's shudder might have indicated a fear of mortality, or of the idea of being found dead in flagrante delicto with Nicky Fontana, or simply of being found dead in a place in which she normally wouldn't be found — well . . . dead.

A smile quirked Nicky's slightly blistered mouth. "We didn't sleep that much. And I told you, those hoods were just trying to scare me."

"Well, they scared me!" Van ran her hands up her naked arms, momentarily forgetting the sheet.

"You should scare more often."

She hid her face in her hands. "It was the brandy," Van moaned.

The red satin rippled as Nicky braced one knee on the bed and took her face in his hands. "I don't care what you call it, Evangeline. It was real."

"And what are you calling me now?"

Nicky grinned. "You were right. Vanessa's no name for you. So I thought and thought, and now I know what you're hiding — Evangeline, like in the poem. Evangeline von Rhine. It's a big moniker for a wispy girl like you; no wonder you shortened it."

"I did not! I was never an E*van*geline or a *Van*essa or a

*Van*ya or whatever ridiculous name you make up for me!"

Before he could answer, a diffident knock sounded on the door, inadvertently pushing it even farther open.

"Now who?" Van hissed. "The entire Sing Song clan? Am I to be paraded like this in front of everyone in Las Vegas?"

Nicky ran to keep the door from yawning further ajar. "Yeah?"

A female hand floated through the opening, trailing a pair of royal-blue high-heeled sandals and several damp pieces of women's clothing.

"Ah . . . Nicky. That whirlpool looks as if you held naval maneuvers in it last night — in the war of the sexes, that is. I only picked up the women's clothing. There was an article of men's attire — one single item — that I left for you to pick up as a matter of principle. Men should learn how to do these things. But your . . . um, guest might appreciate getting these pronto."

"Thanks, Darcy; you're a real sport," Nicky replied sarcastically.

"Sure thing. Twenty minutes should get my leg back in shape, and I'll go. *Ciao* . . ."

Nicky moved back toward the bed, his arms draped like those of a dress-store clerk.

"Someday I'll strangle that girl!" He watched a large, red satin lump burrowing toward the center of the circular bed. "Van, baby, don't take it so hard. She doesn't even know who —"

"But she knows what! Oh, I could die," came the undercover wail.

Nicky unpeeled her like a shiny scarlet grape, only to find her face almost redder than the sheets. Van snatched the damp clothing from his arms.

"At least be a gentleman now and turn your back while I get dressed!"

His dark head shook mournfully as he sat on the mattress edge. "Damn. I wish I had a cigarette, but I haven't carried them for two days — Hey, does that mean I quit smoking?"

He turned for confirmation of this admirable development, but his over-the-shoulder glance met an icy-eyed Van hastily buttoning her wrinkled blue-silk blouse. Nicky turned back to face the heavy red-velvet curtains veiling the windows.

"She'll be gone in a few minutes," he said. "This doesn't have anything to do with what happened last night."

"It has everything to do with it." Dressed at last, if not neatly, Van came around the bed to confront him.

Her hair fell little-girl loose, but her shoulders and face were grimly set. Nicky read a smidgen of regret in her expression, but he was a born optimist. Her next words proved him wrong.

"This just goes to show how . . . inappropriate . . . last night was, Nicky. To us, to our respective positions with the hotel. It can't happen again."

He moved abruptly, but a flash of her open palm, quelling as a traffic cop's, stopped him from speaking.

"Yes, I know it was a stressful evening. We were both scared, hungry, and —"

"Cold?" he interjected bitterly.

"— and carried away. What happened was perfectly natural, under the circumstances. But it doesn't have to become, er, chronic." Every word she chose, trying to be so adult, came out childishly awkward, Van knew. Some raw fear make her talk on, feeling all the while that she was losing her grip on a ladder of silk. "It can't, not while we're working so intensively on the hotel. Business is business and pleasure is —"

"— is nobody's business but ours!"

"Maybe in your world, but not in mine. We'll just pretend it never happened."

She walked to the window to thrust back the ponderous velvet. A beacon of daylight spilled in, turning her blouse electric blue and painting her hair the color of melted butter.

She wouldn't live like her father, Van told herself grimly, hiding behind closed doors, sipping transitory love on the sly. She'd be leaving soon, once the hotel was done and "class" was no longer a critical commodity to Nicky. He was hardly someone to rely upon when it came to enduring emotions — Nicky, who within a week or a month could be telling her the same sensible words of farewell.

"I'm not saying I regret the occurrence —" she said more softly.

"Thanks."

"But we're both adults and can control our whims. And once the project is done, if we should care to . . . revive the relationship, I can't see any harm in an occasional —"

He was beside her ripping the curtains shut. In the heavy shadow his face was fiercer than it had been confronting the thugs in her overlit office the night before. "You say you don't regret it?"

Her expression melted like flame-licked metal as he watched.

"But you'd walk away from it, like . . . that." He snapped his fingers. "Like it was something that didn't matter — some side bet you could afford to lose?"

"Isn't that what men do all the time?" A shadow moved in the room, a shadow from a sand castle Van had smashed long ago. Her voice tautened with fresh control. She'd always been such an adult little girl; it had spared her many disappointments, but not enough. "Really, Nicky, you must learn to separate passion and love. Sometimes you are such a child."

She patted his cheek with icy fingers.

"Yoo-hoo! Anybody home?" Darcy's voice sparkled like sunshine outside the bedroom door. "I'm on my merry way, folks. Thanks again, Nicky. All ye, all ye outs in free, whoever ye be!"

They heard the distant slam of the unmarked door that entered the suite.

"All right," Nicky said slowly, as if he were learning the words and the music to a new song for the first time. "All right. We'll do it your way. You might as well go now. The coast is clear."

At the door she stopped and looked back. "About those men —"

"I'll peel uncle Mario's brain, find out who's muscling in on who nowadays. It happens all the time in Vegas, and it's more bark than bite."

"We still should discuss how we'll increase security, avoid sabotage."

Nicky's waving hand dismissed such a dire possibility. He stood motionless against the lavish red velvet, the lower half of his figure clothed in white, the upper half unclothed bronze. He looked like a severed man, Van thought with an odd pang, as if somebody had cut him in half and he hadn't noticed it yet.

"All right," she agreed. "I'll see you in my office later."

Nicky nodded, not moving, oddly frozen for so vital a personality. Van pulled the door shut behind her, shutting out the disturbing scene, shutting out the gaudy bedroom and tawdry split infinities of self-reflection in its fence of mirrored slats.

Perhaps, she told herself, Nicky was learning to grow up and face the music in a two-faced world. It struck her that she had finally been behind the closed door and that now she was walking away from it, shutting herself out as she had so often been shut out.

"Chef Song!" Van folded her arms and looked dismayed.

The chef raised sheepish eyes as potent as stewed prunes and lowered his cleaver an inch or two. He pointed to the wet sidewalk at the hotel's rear, accompanying the gesture with a string of apparently endless descriptive Chinese syllables.

Van needed no translation. The story was more readable than a pictograph. An irregular wet puddle darkened the aggregate surface. Over it crouched the black cat, huge-eyed as a painting by Keane. In the center of the water lay a beached goldfish, panting visibly.

"— Acapulco Gold —" came two recognizable words in Chef Song's diatribe. Apparently that was the breed of the stranded carp.

"Well, put it back then," Van urged, "before it . . . asphyxiates. At least it's still alive."

Chef Song understood her gestures. He bent, caught the fish on the blunt side of his cleaver and flip it waterward. Wriggling gold vanished beneath a spray of silver droplets. Chef Song's cleaver rotated honed-edge-out . . . toward the vicinity of the cat's magnificent ruff of midnight fur.

"No! If it's hungry we'll feed it. You'll feed it. In the kitchen, and enough so it isn't tempted to snag a fish again."

Chef Song did not understand English, or if he did, he hid it well, but he digested Van's adamant defense of the cat. Growling into his teeth, he held open the glass door while the feline culprit leisurely ambled into the hotel.

Van paused to survey the small niche of nature carved from the hotel's curved side. A week had passed since the night with Nicky. He was adjusting well to the new ground rules, although he'd returned to his outré habit of phantom "smoking."

For once, Van wished she could react with the impulsive vitality that propelled Nicky, that she could do just what she felt like and damn the consequences. But you don't run a hotel on instincts, she told herself once again, you run it with a damn fine eye toward the consequences — of everything, even a roll in the red satin sheets with the playboy of Las Vegas Boulevard.

Convinced once more of her own maturity, Van ambled back into the hotel. The architect from Brazil had come and gone, with his minions, and would return soon with final plans for approval. Before long, the Crystal Phoenix wouldn't be a dream anymore or a deserted hulk sulking on the scintillating Strip but a dazzling reality.

Visualizing the hotel in all its promised dazzle, Van walked through the empty lobby and straight into the arms of a dark-haired youth wearing a pale sports ensemble and a Pepsodent grin.

"Hey, 'scuse me, lady — I didn't see you, for which there is no forgivin' me."

"Shame on you," interjected his clone, who appeared to have popped from behind a pillar. "Are you makin' a pest of yourself again, Ralph? Give the lady some breathin' room and a chance to look at a real man."

"Who're you kidding?" demanded another. "I'm senior

here, kid. Ernesto Fontana at your service, ma'am. I didn't know Nicky had got so smart at keepin' a good thing under his panama."

"This is not whom you think it is," interjected a fourth man, whose mustache lent an almost-thirtyish dignity to the group. "This isn't Nicky's new lady; it's Evonne van Rhine, the new manager, dummies!"

"Aw, Aldo, it is not!" argued one.

"You've got grapes in the *capo,* Aldo," said another.

"Sour grapes," put in the first to greet Van and apparently the second-youngest Fontana brother. This young man bowed to indicate a chair. "Have a seat, Miss Rhine. Those little feet must get tired from being stood on so long."

"I presume I'm speaking to Fontana Incorporated," Van observed as she sat. If Nicky could be a conundrum, a temptation, an irritant, the Fontana boys, *en masse,* took her breath away.

"Oh, no," Ralph answered eagerly. "This is just a few of us. Julio isn't here, or Emilio."

"Or Giuseppe," added Aldo.

"Or Armando," said the middle brother.

"So we're less than half the family, but what's to miss? Eduardo is here." The speaker, evidently the Eduardo in question, smiled modestly.

"And Rico." Another brother bowed to introduce himself.

It didn't matter, Van could no more tell the brothers Fontana apart than she could the siblings Song. All came with sunny good looks, enough energy to raise the Titanic, and quantities of dark hair and flashing white teeth. She couldn't help thinking that Nicky was the best looking of the brothers so far, God forbid that she should meet the rest.

"So this is the Crystal Phoenix!" Aldo, the eldest present, took the measure of the lobby with a blasé face. "It has . . . possibilities." He toyed with the red carnation impaled in the buttonhole of his pale silk-blend Italian suit. With his pencil-thin moustache, he looked like Charlie Chan after a diet.

"So this is the famous Miss von Rhine." At least Ralph got it right, Van thought as he sidled up beside her on the extra wide lounge chair. "Uncle Mario said you were some spicy pepperoni." He shook his fingers as if having just extracted them from a fire. "Mamma mia! Nobody but Mama Tinucci makes uncle Mario back down, and she is dead now." He studied Van as a botanist would eye a rare form of plant life.

Rico perched on the arm of the rapidly overcrowded chair, hands on the knees of his nautically white duck trousers.

"Maybe Nicky's not crazy, after all," he conceded with a wink. He leaned near to Van as she leaned away from his encroaching brothers. "Maybe there's more to the hotel business than we thought."

"Well, it's been charming meeting you all — yes, I know you're not all of the Fontanas, but I'm sure you're a representative sampling. If you'll excuse me, there really are some things I should be attending to in my office."

"What?" they demanded in disappointed chorus.

"The, uh . . ." Van foundered.

"The details." Nicky had dredged up the dead weight of her lost sentence himself, coming up behind her to perch on the chairback, thereby completely hemming her in with Fontanas. "I said I'd like a couple of you boys to drop by now and then. Why the Family excursion?"

He may have been the youngest, but the others answered

with a promptitude that bespoke a certain respect.

"We, uh, just wanted to look over the premises."

"To see what we were guarding," Aldo put in, rolling his eyes romantically at Van.

"If you only wanted a matched pair, Nicky," Ernesto said with fraternal disdain, "you should have asked for Dobermans."

"'Guarding'?" Van twisted to look more directly at Nicky than she had in a week.

"Yeah." He had been toying with the cigarette case, which he'd taken to carrying again, but he dropped it into the side pocket of his light-colored linen blazer. "The boys here are our new security patrol. Less obvious than the normal types and just as discouraging, maybe more so. They're doing me a favor by seeing that nobody messes with me, my hotel, or my classy manager."

On the last words his hands moved lightly to Van's shoulders. She resented the possessiveness of the gesture even as she felt a jolt of adrenaline. Van kept herself still, recognizing that Nicky knew by now how to establish his territory among so large and competitive a brotherhood.

All the smiling faces sobered. "Uncle Mario doesn't know," Ernesto said, making the sentence a statement.

"No," Nicky answered, as if addressing Van only. "I thought it best to keep the Family out of it officially. It's my hotel, my business. But —" He stood, and Van eased back into the chair as she felt the light pressure of his fingers melt away. "— if you guys need some Family seniority to give you bozos permission to visit your little brother —"

"No, Nicky!" "No way, *bambino!*" "No problem," chorused the brothers.

"We're just lost little lambs out for a stroll," Ernesto protested while patting his rear hip significantly.

Van tilted up her face to inquire discreetly of Nicky, "They're not armed, are they?"

Of course they overheard. "Armed?" The very word struck the brothers Fontana with indignation.

"Are you armed, Aldo? Of course not!"

"You, Rico, on our . . . godfather's . . . grave — surely not!"

All protested elaborately.

"Except for me!" Ralph leaned close to Van. She reared away. "I am armed." He held up handsome, square-fingered hands not so meticulously clean beneath the fingernails as Nicky's. "These hands are dangerous weapons. I'm a certified black belt in karate."

Van swallowed as the hands in question flexed demonstratively. "It was so nice meeting you all. I won't worry about the hotel with you four —"

"Nine," Aldo corrected. "All nine of us will be dropping by in turn."

She tried not to look dismayed. "With you nine gentlemen" — they preened in unison — "on the premises."

"I guarantee, Miss von Rhine," Ernesto announced formally, "that not a strand upon your golden head shall be touched by any of the lower elements in Vegas."

"Very . . . reassuring," Van said in farewell, rising, moving quickly across the vast lobby.

At the office hallway she paused. The Fontana boys had swarmed around Nicky and were engaged in inflicting the mock pushes, punches and unselfconscious embraces that marked brothers from a large, noisy and comfortably close family.

Van watched Aldo, the eldest present, aim a fist at Nicky's right cheekbone, where only a fading yellow smudge marked the site of a once gloriously Technicolor black eye. Nicky dodged the pretend blow with youngest-brother tolerance, then suffered the quick, happy hug that followed it.

The brothers Fontana had heard of the assault on one of their own, and were responding. Van was sure she had spotted a lump at the back of Ernesto's suit coat. Armed, no, *signorina*. Not *us* . . . .

She shivered, chilled not only by the thought of pistol-packing violence, but by the cool vastness of the lobby. She felt alone, left out in the cold, and could sense the fraternal warmth radiating from the group across the room as if it were being generated in cruel, deliberate contrast.

As she watched, Nicky turned suddenly from the group. His eyes met hers. Van smiled uncertainly, ashamedly, before turning and walking away.

"So," asked Van, trying not to sound censorious, "how long have you been . . . in your line of work, Mr. Nostradamus?"

The wizened little man chuckled, a sound like popping corn. "Since Methuselah was knee-high to a palfrey, Nostradamus has had *bets* in his belfry." He nodded sagely. "And you don't have to call me Mister, sister; I know I'm just a plain old bookie, cookie."

"But don't your friends call you something . . . uh, for short?"

"The only pet names I ever hear are most unsuitable for the feminine ear," he answered promptly.

Van sat back in the lumpy lobby chair. Evening shadows further disheveled the untidy space. She had just returned from dining at the Flamingo Hilton's twenty-four-hour buffet line — woman doth not live by Song-to-go alone — and now found herself reluctant to return to her room without a dash of before-bedtime human conversation.

Van glanced askance at her undistinguished but poetic companion. She wasn't sure that a rhyming bookie nicknamed Nostradamus qualified as a conversation partner, as Nicky would be the first to tell her.

The elevator doors across the lobby whooshed open. At this point, except for the few nondescript transients who prowled the fringes of the hotel's unoccupied existence, the only hotel staff besides the Song family were the bellboy who fetched and retrieved Van's meal trays and parked Nicky's Vette and the maid who washed the towels and bedsheets, presumably even red satin bedsheets. . . .

The new arrival was none of these, but Nicky Fontana in the flesh, all duded up for a Friday night out on the town. He wore his usual light-color sportcoat over a silk shirt of palest lime that would have looked repellent on anybody else. In the V of its open neck, St. Jude glinted on his chain with impossible twenty-four-carat optimism.

On Nicky's arm clung none other than the dazzling Roxelle, draped in enough rhinestones to make Dolly Parton drool.

An unlit cigarette hung from Nicky's lower lip with the same illusion of levitation as when Van had first laid eyes on him. And Miss Roxelle was still playing femme fatale to the high-heeled hilt, Van thought uncharitably.

The dancer minced over to Van and Nostradamus, dragging a somewhat sheepish Nicky, like Mary's little lamb, behind her.

"Nicky's taking me to the Palace Court at Caesars for dinner, isn't that sweet?"

"Tooth-decaying," Van answered, unable to withdraw her eyes from Roxelle's shoes, this pair pavéd with a literal rainbow of rhinestones. The rainbows that underlined her hyperextended insteps appeared on each heel as well.

"Yeah, well . . . the Palace Court is nothin' special," Nicky put in modestly.

Van raised an eyebrow. She had researched every restaurant in Las Vegas and knew the Palace Court as one of the most costly.

"Here's something, Nicky boy, to help you swallow your dinner," Nostradamus offered, rising and peeling a much-worn leather billfold from his back pocket. "While you eat steak, my wallet grows thinner."

Nicky only grinned as Nostradamus counted five limp hundred dollar bills into his palm.

"Oooh, Nicky, could we go shopping in the Appian Way after dinner? There's a pair of custom-made Eye-talian shoes for only four-ninety-five. . . ."

None present assumed that Roxelle meant four dollars and ninety-five cents.

Nicky carelessly slapped the folded bills into his jacket pocket. "Sure, whatever you want," he said. "At least *you* know what you want."

"What a sweetie!" Roxelle squeezed as close to Nicky as human anatomy would allow and batted her eyelashes, a feat equaling his trick with the cigarette, since Roxelle wore false stage lashes so long and thick that it was a wonder she could keep her eyes open at all.

"I need to consult with you in the morning," Van told Nicky, ignoring Roxelle's swelling pout. "The architect needs a final go-ahead."

"Fine, fine!" In matters of business, Nicky was magnanimous. "I'll stop by your office first thing tomorrow."

He hadn't "stopped by" since the night of . . . Van's thoughts balked, refusing to grant it a title. In the meantime

Roxelle and Nicky were moving to the lobby doors.

"When they say 'ankling,' that's what they mean," Nostradamus mused nostalgically, ogling Roxelle's departure on the flashy wobbling shoes. "They won't replace that with any machine."

"Hmmm." Van tried to remember what she'd meant to ask the bookie. "Nostradamus, about the people who hang around the hotel —"

"They're Vegas types just like yours truly. So ask me no more — I'm no stoolie."

"I wasn't complaining; I simply was wondering who they all are. These anonymous visitors might be dangerous. We've had trouble, you know, with certain people who want us . . . Nicky . . . to give up the hotel."

The little man eyed her sharply. "Danger seldom comes from a stranger's hand. It's when we love that we tread on quicksand."

Van stood. "Honestly, trying to talk with you is like attempting to converse with a . . . a rhyming dictionary! I've a right to know something about what goes on in this hotel! After all, I am the manager!"

She marched to the elevators, certain that *her* retreating ankles weren't being eyed with leering intent. Once aboard, she faced firmly forward, regarding the figure of Nostradamus with unchanged sternness.

The bookie smiled crookedly and not unfondly as the doors closed, then twisted to study his own heels, as if troubled by a haunting pixie. From beneath the lobby chair's moth-eaten skirt wormed a fat black form. Nostradamus stooped to stroke it from head to tail, giving a familiar jerk to the great black tail plume.

"I fear, my friend, that the lady's wary. A sure sign of a heart that's chary. It's in the cards, like trouble tomorrow: Lady Luck's a sure thing compared to Lady Love's certain sorrow."

♣ Chapter Fourteen ♣

"So I'm here," Nicky said.

He stood in front of Van's desk, looking like a defiant schoolboy, impeccably groomed but radiating an air of truancy.

Van glanced at the flat full moon of Swiss gold on her wrist.

"Yeah, I know it's one o'clock." Nicky's knees suddenly buckled, and he sat hastily on the spare visitor's chair, not even noticing the overstuffed monstrosity in the corner that Van kept only because he seemed to favor it.

Seed pearls of sweat glistened on his forehead; the healthy summer bronze of his skin had tarnished to green.

"Are you all right?" Van, concerned, was standing, but Nicky waved her back into her seat again.

"Fine. I just had a big night out on the town last night," he explained with a flare of his usual bravado.

"Oh." The word, short as it was, came out pinched, as if it had been marinated in lemon recently. Until then, Van had successfully expunged the distasteful image of Nicky and Roxelle from her mind.

He read her thoughts, then shrugged his surrender to the truth.

"I got in at midnight — some night on the town. I left Roxelle off early and mostly walked the Strip — smoking." His face curdled. "I must have smoked a whole pack!" His shoulders shuddered as he rubbed his face in his hands. "I think I'm cured." He peeked up between careful fingers. "Of cigarettes."

"Then I imagine the idea of lunch" — Nicky made an ungentlemanly noise — "doesn't appeal to you, so we might as well tour the hotel."

He nodded docile agreement and followed her into the lobby. "I know what's planned for the major areas," he said. "I really don't see why you wanted to lead this little sightseeing expedition."

"I want you to keep abrea— current with everything that's happening," Van said. "After all, it's your hotel."

"I guess." Nicky shoved his hands in his pants pockets and studied the floor as the tip of his cream-leather loafer made idle patterns on it.

Van, observing this uncharacteristic indifference, sighed, bridled, and then straightened.

"We'll begin with the carpeting, since it intrigues you so much. As I mentioned, Montero is one of the most innovative architects in Brazil. And both Rio and Brazilia boast a spectacular architecture style geared for a hot, tourist-oriented area, like Las Vegas.

"Montero's going along with our glassed-in outer waterway concept, and his interior designers have honed our approach. The carpet, instead of the commonplace red-and-black that haunts most Las Vegas hotels — maybe because it echoes the color of gambling chips — will be a custom-woven deep burgundy and navy color, with an Oriental medallion design of a phoenix on a solid ground. The phoenix motif will repeat itself on the hotel linens, the doors to the suites — in fact the peephole will be the phoenix's eye — the towels, bedding, major door hardware, bathroom fixtures, bath mats, and so on."

Nicky nodded. "I get it; 'motifs' are classy, and burgundy-and-navy is the next thing to red-and-black, but . . . nicer somehow."

"Subtler," Van elaborated. "Less predictable. There's good reason for the traditional Las Vegas decor. Red and black represent richness, away-from-home elegance; it's the most successful restaurant color scheme. The Crystal Phoenix will draw from the familiar, but transmute it. There will be touches of the Chinese, the contemporary, the commercial. It will offer a kind of architectural alchemy, an oasis of elegant entertainment."

"To the tune of eight million bucks," Nicky noted ruefully.

"Seven and a quarter million bucks," she corrected. "You're still spending seven hundred and fifty thousand to remodel your penthouse, aren't you?"

"Yeah, sure . . ." He spoke as if just remembering the project. "Why not? Why shouldn't I have *that* the way I like it?"

"I'm not saying you shouldn't. It's budgeted in." Van frowned and looked down at the Plexiglas clipboard she held pressed against her chest. "Nicky, don't you care about the hotel anymore? Have you lost interest . . . already?"

"No! It's just that you — Montero, the interior designers — have it under control. Everything's in motion, like a train on a track. The Van von Rhine Line. What's left for Nicky Fontana to worry about except some local muscle? I seem to be —"

"Superfluous?"

He looked at her with a weary, tolerant smile. "I wouldn't have put it that way. I was going to say dead weight. Excess baggage."

She bristled defensively. "You're the man with the money."

"I know. That doesn't seem to be enough, the way it used to be. Look, the hotel's shaping up swell. It's more than I ever dreamed it would be, more than I ever could dream it to be. So take the seven hundred and fifty grand and spread it around down here where it'll do some good. I'll fix up my joint from a little dough I got tucked away."

He turned for the elevators.

"What about . . . our tour? Aren't you going to see how the rest of the hotel is planned?"

He paused and glanced back briefly before the stainless steel doors snapped shut on him. "Surprise me."

After Nicky had left, Van stood alone, studying the empty lobby, absently ruffling the lackadaisical carpeting with the toe of her pump. Her clipboard held a thick sheaf of design plans, every page freckled with notations flagging matters yet to be settled.

As she had warned Nicky, the hotel under reconstruction would soon resemble a combat zone, inside and out. Making the last choices, setting the details should be the most enjoyable part of the process.

"It should be *fun,*" she told the hooded machines, the leafless palms, the cigarette-butt-laden ashtrays, and empty lounge chairs. None of them answered.

She retraced her steps, visible among the dusty litter of the untended carpet, to the office. There, upon her desk, perched like a sultan from an episode of the *Arabian Nights,* sat the black cat.

Van went behind her desk and pulled out a drawer, hunting some filling she had saved from the tuna fish sandwich she'd had for lunch, much to Chef Song's dismay. Paper napkins were forbidden to Chef Song's trays, and Van had forgotten to save the cloth one. She moved the warming glop from her empty paper-clip box to the palm of her hand.

"Here you go, fellah. You, at least, have some manners and don't sulk under the desk all day simply because you can't have your way with me."

The cat eased onto its well-padded haunches and ate with fastidious efficiency, pausing now and again to lathe her wrist approvingly with the rough side of its tongue.

Van's free hand stroked the lowered forehead, where the fur was short and velvet-smooth. "At least you're grateful!" It began purring as if on cue.

She glanced over her shoulder to the clutter of her desk. In too short a time she would be chained behind that desk as legions of workers invaded the building and reshaped it to her plans. The thought should have been exciting and highly satisfying. Instead, she only felt an aimless restiveness, a sense of something slipping away even as a greater something loomed into reality.

"Nice kitty," Van crooned to the cat licking up the last tuna flakes seasoned by the salt of her palm. If only Nicky Fontana came so domesticated.

The cobalt-silk blouse was hanging from the doorknob to her room when Van finally returned to it at eight-thirty that evening after another solitary dinner out.

It startled her, resembling a vivid ghost of itself as it shook subtly in the unseen draft from an air-conditioning vent. She paused to stare at it, abandoning her reverie only when some faint sound — or motion — caught her attention.

She whirled. The silver-haired man was returning to his room, too, and it was adjacent to hers — amazing to think that they had never run into one another before. . . .

But apparently he knew her. His head nodded as he passed through his door and a slim smile — not recognition so much as the kind of smile meant for a fellow conspirator — settled on his thin lips. He looked like a man who often smiled to himself, and had been doing it for a long, long time.

Van smiled back; she couldn't help herself. How silly she was, to let the sight of a simple blouse shake her. Her neighbor had vanished behind his door, but she felt a fresh need to put up a good front — for herself if no one else.

The blouse was there because it had been dry cleaned, as she had requested, and was now being mutely returned. Every reminder from the evening that nagged at her composure was slipping back into pristine, pre-Nicky condition.

Everything, thought Van, whisking the hanger off the knob and entering her room, except me.

She turned on the television while preparing for bed, hung up the blouse, exchanged her work clothes for a nightgown of silver-gray silk, and curled up on the conventionally rectangular double bed. A glance at the ceiling confirmed that neither leprous-looking strips of mirror nor red velvet lurked above her soon-to-be-dreaming head.

Van turned off the television early, telling herself she had a lot of paperwork to do tomorrow, and slid between the white sheets, the familiar feel of hotel-grade cotton-and-polyester bed linens smooth on her cheek.

Visions of the Crystal Phoenix's revamped guest rooms danced in her head with sugar-plum sweetness: a navy, burgundy, and cream color scheme, with new amenities in every unit — wall-mounted hair dryers, bathroom-ceiling heat lamps, phones in both bedroom and bath. . . .

One such phone was ringing now with most undreamlike insistence. Van dredged herself out of the bed linens to pick up the bedside phone. The luminous clock dial read ten forty-five.

"Yes?"

"It's Nicky. Listen. Brother Ralph was prowling the lobby and thought he saw signs of somebody poking around. Are you all right?"

"I *was* all right," she told him. "I was sleeping."

"Your door's locked?"

"Of course! I didn't grow up in hotels for nothing."

"And no one's been lurking around?"

"Nicky, I haven't seen a soul all day except for that stray black cat and the poor old man who lives next door to me, and he hardly looks like hired muscle."

Nicky's voice tightened. "What old man?"

"I don't know, some silver-haired duffer; stooped. I've noticed him before. Don't you even know who does the dirty work around this place? I supposed he was the gardener or something. He looks as if he'd enjoy outdoor work — something about his sun-seamed face. . . ."

"Van, I have a service handle all that and the pool. And I don't employ —" Nicky's voice stopped.

"Nicky? Are you there? Is something wrong?" She sat up. Maybe somebody *was* in the hotel. Maybe while Nicky had been worrying about *her,* they'd been stalking *him.* "Nicky!"

"Hey. Calm down." His voice thickened and warmed with the old Fontana charm. "I, uh, think I'll run down and check, just to make sure. Don't unlock your door until I get there."

Her hands tightened on the receiver. "I'm not sure I'll unlock it when you get here."

Silence, followed by a gusty sigh. "I'm not kidding, Van. Just sit tight, and I'll be right there. Don't open the damned door until then, and then open it, no matter what you want to prove to me."

He paused again and then spoke quickly, flatly, finally. "There's nobody legit booked next door to you. I arranged

154

it specially, so the new manager could have his privacy from the domestic staff. There's not supposed to be anybody in that whole end of the seventh floor. You should have the place completely to yourself."

He hung up without a good-bye, leaving Van clinging to a droning dial tone and the realization that she might not be as utterly alone as she had thought she was, which was cold comfort under the circumstances.

The clock was a digital model, its bright red numbers dancing through the normal one-to-ten sequence. She would have preferred watching a second hand spin slowly round and round. It was somehow more comforting to watch time pass in the hairline-thin progress of a gilt wand than to see it jerk from minute to minute in a numerical St. Vitus dance.

She got up and found an aqua terry cloth robe — street length, strictly for travel and utterly incongruous over the long gown — but she was cold and Nicky Fontana was coming.

She put on slippers and even combed her hair, studying her pale face in the bathroom mirror. Why couldn't danger do the decent thing and raise its ugly head before a lady had consigned her daily mask to the wastepaper basket? Not that Nicky Fontana would care; he seemed intent on proving how little he cared about anything nowadays.

She went to stare out the main room windows at the black panorama of night lit by the soft, syncopated glow from the combined candlepower of lights magnified into the billions and billions, like Carl Sagan's stars on *Cosmos*, all pulsing rhythmically.

The knock on the door startled her, like anything expected for too long. She peered through the peephole, remembering the first night he had stood outside her door, the night they toured the Strip.

Nicky exploded into the room as soon as Van unlatched the chain, looking around as if for a phantom lover.

"You okay?"

She nodded. "But what — ?"

"Shhhh!" One hand was on her lips. The other held a gun.

"Nick-y!" she protested.

"Take it easy. Better this than not. And keep your voice down; these walls are rice paper. I told you, nobody's supposed to be around here, period. You've got a prowler."

"Maybe it's some old vagrant who slipped in when no one was looking. There are panhandlers even in Las Vegas."

"Yeah. And they're down on the Strip panhandling at this hour. It's their prime shift. Now cut the palaver. You say this guy went in next door?"

"It looked like it."

Nicky flashed a passkey. "I went downstairs and got this."

"That's what took you so long."

He grinned suddenly. "Did you miss me?"

"No! I just sat here doing my nails!"

"And that's what you can do while I go next door . . . what's this room? — oh, yeah, seven-eleven. Lucky number."

Her hand clutched his arm. "Nicky — the next room is seven-thirteen!"

"So?"

"Don't you know what day it is?"

"Not according to my Family and certain hotel managers I know."

"Well, I do know, because I work in an office and have a desk calendar. Nicky — today is Friday the 13th!"

"So?"

"So don't go next door now; it's unlucky."

"I don't believe in luck either way, honey, bad or good. I'll take an equalizer any day." He hefted the pistol.

"That's even unluckier."

"If I don't come back or knock on the wall in a few minutes, call the police."

"Can't you call your brothers first?"

"And look like a fool if it's just an empty room? No thanks."

"You'd die to save face in front of your brothers?"

His hand clamped her forearm. "Nobody's going to die. This old dude sounds like a pushover even Nostradamus could handle. Just sit tight, and I'll be back in a minute or two."

He turned for the door.

Van jumped up, hurtled across the room and glued herself to his back. "I'm going with you. It's my job! And besides, I'll go crazy if I have to sit alone here any longer — wondering. And" — it was a blatant appeal to his macho heritage — "I'm probably safer with you."

He finally nodded. "All right. But stay behind me. And get ready to rabbit back to the room and call the cops — with me or without me — if anything goes wrong."

Van nodded doubtful agreement to this unpalatable scenario. Slowly, Nicky pushed open the door. He soft-footed his way into the hall.

Van, as agreed, kept well behind him, inching along the opposite side of the wall. Enough light fell from the closest dim sconce to illuminate the brass numbers on her neighboring door — seven-thirteen. Seven-one-three, she thought, which added up to eleven, which equaled the last two digits in her room number!

She scanned the dark hallway for signs of the black cat,

relieved that at least that four-legged omen had shown the good taste to remain elsewhere.

Nicky crept down the hall, pausing at the closed door. Van felt five years old again. She was watching her father, it seemed, move beyond one of those closed doors forbidden to her, one of those doors from which he'd at last never emerged alive again.

Then the present overlaid the past, and she saw Nicky slip the key into the lock, thrusting the gun into the back of his belt as he turned the knob. He moved as silently as a second-story man, no doubt an inbred Fontana talent, Van thought rather unfairly. The door to seven-thirteen split open a few unrevealing inches.

For a moment, Van thought she saw the glitter of Lady Death behind that narrow, black bar of empty air. She wanted to rush forward and warn Nicky, but he was easing the chrome pistol from his belt and holding up a cautionary hand. She could only hold her peace, cling to the cold hallway wall, and wait.

Nicky had slipped through the slot of darkness and closed the door behind him, so no light from the hall should leak in. Oh, he was good at this sort of thing, Van thought, as good as a TV detective. Perhaps he had missed his calling. He was in the room alone for a long time, five minutes or so, and in that time Van saw or heard nothing.

Then the thin line of darkness soundlessly flared into the white of a lamp-lit room. Van pushed herself away from the wall, ready to rush back to her room, or into the unknown room.

The white light fattened, and Nicky stepped through it into the hall, the gun held carefully yet casually in his hand high on the opening door.

"False alarm. Nobody here. Looks like nobody's been

here since 1945. Come on in, Van. You won't believe your eyes. This is outa sight!"

Unlike most of Nicky Fontana's assertions, this one promised to be a massive understatement.

♣ Chapter Fifteen ♣

"You ever seen anything *like* this joint?" Nicky demanded.

He set his gun on a mahogany side table beside a lamp whose dusty cream-silk shade was decoratively laced down one side in perfect imitation of a nineteenth-century corset.

Van crossed the threshold like a sleepwalker, forgetting that this very room had frightened her not moments before. What she saw erased every emotion but wonder.

Time-dusted furniture crouched in every corner of what was obviously the living room of a suite. On their spindly eighteenth-century-style curved supports, the chairs and tables looked like a convention of Daddy Longleg spiders.

"Mahogany, right?" Nicky asked. "Ever see anything like it?"

"Only at the Algonquin Hotel on Forty-fifth Street in New York City. This is original 1940s decor."

"But it's first-class stuff?"

"First class."

Nicky nodded and sank onto an overstuffed chintz armchair, complete with skirt. He looked as misplaced as a bull in a florist shop, and just as oblivious to his surroundings.

"The Joshua Tree was built around 1945," he said, "in the postwar building boom Bugsy Siegel started that made Vegas into the hot town it is today." He glanced around with winning deference. "What I know about decor you could put in Montero's front tooth cap, but this is real wild stuff."

"This is incredible." Van moved through the room, dusting her fingertips over faded upholstery and along the grimy slats of painted wood venetian blinds. Above the cumbersome blinds loomed upholstered satin valances with their corners curled into shapes resembling the upswept coils of pomaded hair on femme fatales in 1940s films. "The color scheme alone is priceless —"

"Yeah, what do they call that shade of green?" Nicky pointed at the wallpaper, a black bamboo design etched on a background of pure . . .

"Chartreuse," Van answered promptly, using the French pronunciation.

Nicky's aquiline nose twitched its distaste. "When I was a kid, I used to call it slime-green. Anyway, when I first came in, I poked my nose — and the Beretta's — into every nook, cranny, and closet in this suite. There's no seedy old gent to be seen. Just more of this funky furniture."

"Obviously, the suite was decorated originally for a resident guest. She — or he — must have lived here since the Joshua Tree opened."

"Hey!" Nicky's fingers snapped smartly as he lurched forward in the froufrou-laden chair. "I bet this was Jersey Joe's setup! He was a small-time Howard Hughes, sort of. Anyway, he kept to himself and lived at the Joshua Tree. The word was he'd been rich once, only nobody knew how or why. I think he croaked" — Van stared at him uncomprehendingly — "the old coot kicked off about the time the hotel changed hands eight years ago. They probably just planted him — by then he didn't have a dime to phone home with, I heard — and left the rooms alone. Nostradamus'd know. Just think; Jersey Joe's original digs. . . ." Nicky settled back, content to have assigned the suite an owner.

"Charming story." Van moved into the adjoining bedroom. " 'Jersey Joe' must have had some . . . dough . . . because this stuff wasn't cheap, even then. Will you look at the satin spreads on the twin beds? Jersey Joe must have had a Jersey Jenny in his life once."

"A lot of characters hung out around Vegas back then — you know, colorful types."

Van turned to regard Nicky, who had come to stand in the doorway, looking as colorful as could be in a turquoise knit sport shirt and cream pants, with the gold medal blinking its optimistic message neon-bright against his tanned chest.

But Nicky was looking back at Van just as intently. The bizarre surroundings twisted them both into sharper focus, as if they saw each other more clearly in an alien environment.

"Where'd you get that wrapper?" he asked. "It looks like it belonged to Minnie the Moocher's mother." Nicky's tone was amused, but uncritical. "You look like you should be wearing hair curlers."

"I don't, ever," Van defended herself. "That's why I wear my hair up."

"No curlers." Nicky nodded thoughtfully. "A girl like that could grow on a guy."

Van suddenly wished she hadn't quenched the sleek luxury of her gown under such a homely overlay. Nicky's expression was changing, indicating that it, too, wished something was not the way it was.

At that instant, a horrendous thump rang from the living room. Nicky's expression of regret screwed into instant self-blame. "The gun's on the table!" he whispered, turning to face whoever lurked behind him.

Van ran for the doorway too, knowing she shouldn't have.

They confronted an empty room. No visible trace of what had caused the harsh noise remained, not even a swaying blind or a swinging door. They prowled the room's perimeter, slowly, as if wading through waist-high mud, as if expecting to encounter some unseen obstacle more palpable than their own confusion.

"Something must have moved," Van declared.

"Some*one*," Nicky corrected grimly, arming himself again.

But he could find nothing to aim at but emptiness and faded furniture. He finally lowered the gun barrel, shaking his head at the lurid walls. "Chartreuse. . . ."

"It was highly fashionable," Van insisted, "at the time." She opened the center drawer of a Sheraton desk against one wall. "Was Jersey Joe's last name Jackson?"

"That's it!" Nicky sprinted to the desk and hung over her, his closeness pressing the rough terry cloth robe to her shoulder blades. "That must be the old dude's bank book. Hezekiah Joseph Jackson . . . no wonder they called him Jersey Joe. Man, his account was flat as Irontop Mesa when he blew out. Not a peso in it! They must have buried him on the county and forgot all this. Crazy, isn't it?"

"Not so crazy. There's the thump."

Nicky's eyes followed Van's pointing finger to the wall behind the desk. A large canvas of some kind leaned behind it. On the wallpaper above the green-shaded desk lamp, a large rectangle outlined an acidic blotch of unfaded chartreuse.

"Off the wall!" Nicky declared. "It let loose and fell off the wall after all this time." He groaned while leaning down to wrestle the canvas free. "Hey, it's a blow-up photo. You want to see what Las Vegas looked like before the war?" Nicky stretched to hook the work on its rusted hangers and stepped back.

"Once a wasteland, always a wasteland," Van noted,

studying the black-and-white aerial photo of what seemed an endless desert undistinguished by signs of any living creature other than a wild burro and a blur of rocks that assumed the shape of a camel. "That's a strange, officelike thing to hang in a place decorated like this."

"Some people like the desert," Nicky said pointedly. "Some people like to see the stars and sniff the sagebrush. If you came to Vegas back in the thirties, before air-conditioning, you had to like the desert, believe me!"

"I believe you." Van looked around again with a cool, professional eye. "I don't know what we'll do with this suite; maybe simply lock it up and forget it. I could have sworn —"

"Look." Nicky took her by the aqua-terry cloth shoulders and kneaded them as if reaching for the muscles beneath. "You've been working hard lately, and living like a hermit in that suite next door. The hotel's semideserted except for all these characters around the place who have the mistaken idea that I won't mind if they come and go as they please. So it's my fault. This isn't a normal place, Van, and won't be again until it's redone and filled with people and singing slot machines and live music and laughter and Lady Luck."

His voice was almost hypnotic. "Maybe that's why we get on each other's nerves," he continued.

Nicky Fontana in a state of sweet reason grated on her. She tried to shrug away his hands. "That's not why! It has nothing to do with this hotel or my fatigue or your intentions."

"What has it got to do with?" he asked soberly.

"Us!"

Nicky's massaging hands dropped from her shoulders. "I didn't think there *was* an 'us,' just an 'indiscretion.' "

"There is and you know it!" Van sat on the sofa, which

was upholstered in a fabric featuring huge leaves of forest green, rose, gray and chartreuse. She sank into the design as if swallowed by a rotting Technicolor jungle. "I have *tried* to ignore it!"

"What're you ignoring so hard? Me?"

"Not you, I don't blame you. You can't help being . . . I blame — it."

"It." Nicky sat beside her, laying the gun on the low glass-topped coffee table butting against their knees.

Van felt confused, he realized, and afraid of getting hurt, like someone bumping around in a strange room in the dark. That was exactly what they both were doing, he understood suddenly. They were cracking their shins on each other and cursing the darkness.

"Just forget it," she was saying. "You're right. I'm exaggerating —"

"No, you're not. This place — the Joshua Tree or the Crystal Phoenix or whatever you call it — is bad for you. I'm bad for you."

"No!" She looked more horrified than when the photograph had fallen moments before. Then her voice gentled. "No . . . you're not bad for me."

"Then the hotel is!" His voice was so rough it surprised him. "Why?"

When she answered, she stared straight ahead as if on a witness stand. "I grew up in hotels. I was even born in one. All I know is hotels. I thought that's all I could do . . . something with hotels. Maybe I was wrong, because I wasn't ever happy in hotels."

"Why not?" Nicky almost whispered now. Once she started talking she had begun a monologue; he just had to make encouraging noises now and again to keep it going.

"Oh, I suppose when I was a child it was my father. He wasn't an affectionate man, at least not to children, and we lived in such an adult world. And then, when I got . . . older —"

She stopped, her fingers rolling the terry-cloth robe into a washclothlike wad on her knees, the kind of thing a little girl does when she's put in front of a camera and has to keep smiling from the neck up while her knees are knocking.

"So what about me bothers you?" Nicky persisted.

"Everything! You're so carefree and optimistic and . . . engaging and irresponsible —"

"Hey, I may play the good-time Charlie, but this hotel is a big responsibility; I put more work into it than shows. How do you think I got the consortium together to buy the building in the first place — all legit Vegas business types? That's why I got a college degree in business administration. I'm responsible to them for the good use of more dough than Mama Tinucci ever wrapped around a pepperoni in her wildest dreams.

"So I don't know chartreuse from puce. Nobody's going to scare me off this hotel — not hoodlums and not a classy ice cube from the Old-World side of the Atlantic Ocean."

"I'm not an ice cube! And besides, how could I, a poor little orphan, scare a big-time Vegas operator like you away from the Crystal Phoenix? Why would you even think that?"

"Because you damn near have since . . . that night."

Her face shifted through several expressions he had seen before: shock, denial, icy pride. It finally settled on one he had never seen before. He instantly christened it Haute Surprise.

"It was that bad?"

Nicky brought his face so close, it almost touched hers, a trick his uncle Mario performed when he wanted to make sure that someone understood him perfectly.

"It was that *good*."

"Oh." She flushed and suddenly released the furrows of mangled fabric on her knees. "Then what's the problem?"

"You!" Nicky got up to pace. "You just turned off, like one of those damn peacock faucets in my damn over-decorated bathroom! You made me feel like something in bad taste. Like you thought I wasn't worth bothering about — maybe a kick to go slumming with, but nobody to get too close to. Who cares what the bedroom scenery's like when you're making love?"

"I'm sorry! I was surprised, that's all. I hadn't seen where I was until I woke up and I certainly didn't expect to wake up there. Is that why you seem uninterested in the hotel remodeling now? It reminds you of me?"

"It seems cold, calculated, expensive. If that reminds me of you, then that's it." Nicky turned his back on the room, studying the almost abstract black-and-white monotony of photograph-frozen desert.

"I'm not . . . that way. I've got a good head for business, and I like to keep my feelings under control but —"

"Why?" Nicky asked.

"Well, it makes for a smoother-functioning world. Mature people can't get things done without managing their feelings."

"You call that mature? I call that having no fun fast. Van — oh, what's the use?" Nicky strode to the open door.

"And" — something in her voice stopped him — "and people can't use you, if you control your feelings. They can only hurt you if you thrust your feelings right out there in plain view to be seen and mauled . . . and walked out on."

"I know."

She came up behind him. "Nicky. I didn't do that to you." He was silent. "I couldn't have. You have nothing to lose."

He wheeled, then dammed whatever words or gestures wanted to push out of him. He leaned against the doorjamb, deceptively relaxed, his head tilted back to rest on the frame.

"Okay. I started it. It's my nature. Maybe I'm not mature. I act on what I feel. I knew you were . . . well, not my type, but I went for it anyway. So I started it. But you finished it. 'Very nice, Mr. Fontana. Quite an amusing evening, although the ambiance was too-too tacky. We must do it again sometime, but not too soon or too often. Wouldn't want these outings to become habit-forming or anything, nooo.' "

"I gave you your freedom! Isn't that what men want — women who don't tie them down, who are accused of trying to turn every natural urge into unnatural bondage? I said we could . . . someday, maybe . . . get together again."

"Van . . ." He ran impatient hands down her arms, stared as deep into the defensive cobalt shoals of her eyes as he could get. He enunciated every word. "I don't want to know what you *think* men want. I want to know what you want. I want to know if you want me!"

She swallowed. He could see tears sheening her eyes. "That's a very impolite thing to ask a lady."

"I'm not a gentleman."

She smiled suddenly. "Yes, you are; you just don't know it."

"Don't you care if we never get any closer than this again? Don't you care if we turn this hotel into a palace and we're the loneliest people in it?"

"Lonely?" She wanted to deny the word, Nicky thought,

to deny his right to use the word. "How can *you* talk about loneliness? You have that huge family who adores you. You have bookies and vagrants and chorus girls in your hip-pocket. You have money and security and enough confidence to sell the Brooklyn Bridge to . . . to the Kremlin! Don't pretend you need me —"

Nicky's hands tightened. "What if I did? What if I did need you — and there was nobody there. If there was just another vacant room?"

Van glanced down at his grip — half custodial, half homicidal. Nicky fanned his hands free as if to prove he didn't need to touch her.

She turned back to the sofa, sitting in the exact middle of the long cushions, making herself approachable and absolutely unapproachable at the same time.

It was what was driving him crazy, Nicky reflected, the way she drew him and repelled him, the way his heart went out to her and then hit hard on the invisible barrier of her tightly closed emotional front door.

"I'm . . . careful." She folded her hands on her lap, company-manners style. "I don't want to . . . impede . . . anyone by becoming overly dependent, by making a scene. Would you be happier if I camped on your front doorstep, if I challenged your girlfriends to mud wrestling matches in Caesars Palace? If I lost all my dignity?"

"I like your dignity." He stood by the coffee table, which formed a once-modish moat between them. "And I like you when you lose your dignity even better," he added mischievously, unable to resist.

This time she didn't flush. She didn't even answer.

"I'm not your father, Van," Nicky went on seriously. "You don't have to stay out of my way. You don't have to 'spare me' yourself."

Her chin trembled infinitesimally. All the warmth in Nicky strained to leap over the cocktail table and enfold her in his empathetic arms. Poor little orphan. Her sarcastic self-analysis had been too astute. She was indeed an orphan, consigned to hotel hirelings and shadowy back halls by a father too awkward to do more than tolerate a kid, he thought bitterly, and then knew he could never understand such rejection. Nicky held himself back, waiting.

"Perhaps not, although my father died of love I didn't see and certainly never felt. But it isn't just my father." If she'd had a handkerchief, her hands would have been wringing it. Instead, she rubbed them together as if warming her fingertips.

"There was a man — once. I was just nineteen and we were in Munich then — at an ultra-modern hotel there. My father preferred a more traditional hotel, but he was, after all, German and thought he could feel at home there. Gerd was his assistant manager. He paid attention to me, which my father didn't notice —"

Nicky let an impolite sound escape.

"Gerd was very logical, very ambitious. Somehow he managed to charm me. He took me up to the rooftop one night, with a magnum of champagne —"

"Brandy's better," Nicky said sardonically.

She looked up, startled.

"For rooftop seductions. Go on."

His self-deprecating humor had helped. She met his eyes as she talked now and got right to the ugly heart of the matter.

"It was champagne — that time. Gerd 'plied' me with it, I think is the expression. I was a child still. He seduced me. I thought I loved him. Then I found out who he really was courting when I overheard some of the maids gossiping.

170

The hotel. My father. He wanted to become manager when my father moved on — as Gerd knew he would — as my father always did. Gerd would have married me, I think."

She looked down at her twined, ring-bare hands. Nicky realized he'd never seen so much as a friendship ring on her little pinkie.

"But I found out. So when my father left, as he always did, he took me with him, as he always did. Gerd became manager anyway. I had been just so much . . . overkill."

"Gerd was a creep," Nicky said flatly.

Van laughed. "Among other things."

"It could have been worse," he consoled. "You could have married the bastard."

" 'Bastard.' " Her lips tasted the word as she said it. "I like that. I never thought of him that way."

"It always helps to have somebody else call 'em bastards for you," Nicky explained casually. "So what has all this to do with me?"

"I just wanted you to know that it's all right."

"That what's all right?"

"The . . . the other night. It was just something that happened. I don't expect anything more out of it. I got over that. I'm a big girl now. I don't blame you, and you shouldn't blame me. It doesn't have to lead to anything or pretend to be anything more than it was."

Nicky squatted across from her, staring at her gravely over the cocktail table. "What was it?"

"A mutual . . . sensual . . . encounter, I suppose. I don't regret it, I'm even flattered —"

"Well, I'm not!" Nicky thundered. His dark eyes narrowed. "How dare you, Van von Rhine? Where do you get off, thinking of me as a casual lay? As somebody you can turn on and off. One-night stands aren't my style."

Van's mouth opened as wide as her eyes. She looked like a cartoon character drawn in a state of mesmerized shock.

"I — I'm being very reasonable. You should be grateful," she sputtered. "What about those chorus girls you have running in and out of here day and night?"

"Darcy's a pal. I went to high school with her, for Chrissake! And Roxelle — well, she's a lot of fun, a very funny girl. I like her. It wasn't until you came along that I started seeing that maybe I was interested in something different, something more. I got aspirations, Van, give me credit for that."

She looked down at her tightly enfolded fingers. "I'm facade, Nicky — a European education, a certain sense of instilled style. You call it class, but that's not much to aspire to. You've got more class than everyone listed in Debrett's *Peerage* put into one big blue-blooded ball."

Nicky's hands reached across the glass tabletop to cover hers. He rose, drawing her around the coffee table to his side with one hand, an innately classy motion not unlike that in a long-ago gavotte.

Tears glossed Van's eyes, too proud to fall, making their blueness marble-bright, not a first-class comparison, Nicky knew, but then he'd never claimed to have a way with words. Her fingers felt as cold as the ice in the bottom of an empty Old-fashioned glass.

"Now," Nicky said sternly, "I don't think you should stay alone tonight, after this scare, and I certainly don't want to. So we can go back up to my place, or next door to yours. If you say so, I won't lay a glove on you. If you don't, you can expect first-class fingering and lots of it. I don't apologize for that, and you don't apologize if I happen to decide I like you and we should do this more often."

She was ready to cling to him, but still reluctant enough

to argue. "Nicky, this complicates everything."

"Not everything, just our crummy little corner of the world. We can handle it," he promised, bending to kiss her wet eyelashes.

Her arms convulsively clasped his body, her upturned lips brushing the rough side of his shaven cheek.

"Nicky, you're impossible," she whispered.

He moved finally to take from her lips the wordless message he trusted more than talk. The photograph behind them crashed to the floor, and they turned, a bit late but still startled, to face it.

"I'll hang the damn thing up so good it'll stay there until Doomsday." Nicky moved toward it.

"No!"

He paused, eyebrows raised. "No?"

"It's bad luck to rehang the same picture twice."

"It is? I never heard that one."

"Leave it; I'll have it moved to my office in the morning."

Nicky looked even more confused.

"As a souvenir," Van explained. "Of tonight. Unless you think," she added provocatively, "that it won't be worth remembering."

"Tell me," Nicky begged, drawing featherweight fingers along Van's shoulder.

"No." She giggled girlishly. "No way."

"Tell me," he insisted softly. Then his eyes spoke for him. "Trust me."

She sobered instantly. "It's . . . it's —"

"Come on, spit it out, or I'll resort to torture." His fingers drummed lightly along her bare sides.

"That's not torture, Nicky. If you want to talk real torture. . . ."

"I give up," Nicky swore ardently. "You're killing me. But tell me your real name before I die."

"I thought the *victim* was supposed to confess?"

"Yeah, you're a little rule keeper, aren't you?" Nicky responded with deeper kisses until Van's warm body shivered beside his. "Warning's fair; I break rules. And I ferret out names. Tell me."

"You'll laugh."

"Not . . . doing this, I won't."

"Oh. Oh, oh, oh, Nicky!"

"Oh . . . but I have no name yet."

"Vanilla!"

"Huh?"

"No, don't stop. Oh, that's wonderful. Vanilla. That's it. My name."

He stopped. "It's a pudding!"

"And an ice cream and a color and the bean of a South American orchid — and my name."

Nicky rolled onto his side to take a new look at her. "Where'd you get it?"

"From my mother. Nanny said she was American and whimsical. Nanny was British, and of course neither approved of being American or whimsical."

"Va-nill-a." Nicky let the word loll lazily on his tongue. "I like it. It's a very . . . consuming sort of word. But is it tasteful?" he teased.

"Absolutely not! That's why I never use it."

"Never say never, Vanilla. Umm, just right, smooth and creamy."

"I'm sure that's not what my mother had in mind."

"Who knows what she had in mind? I don't think she

would have wanted you to be Van von Rhine."

"I don't know what she wanted for me. Sometimes I hardly know what *I* want for me."

Nicky sat up in the tangled sheets. They were in Van's bedroom, where they had elected to go more from urgency than choice. The fright that had reunited them had been forgotten. Jersey Joe Jackson had been permanently installed in their minds as a bizarre, benign fairy godfather in absentia. If he hadn't been a creature of his times and subscribed to twin beds, they might have mussed the long-ago made-up linens in the room next door.

"I like it here now," Van said, staring at the softly lit ceiling where the bright shadows of Las Vegas's neon fireworks danced. "The room didn't feel . . . loved in . . . before."

She prepared to blush in the dusky light, but Nicky was there before the boldness of the new thought could sink in. He seemed endlessly capable of blending sex and affection, eroticism and fondness. Van felt embraced on every level when she made love with Nicky.

"Oh, baby," he whispered. "You are a Vanilla thrill-ah."

Her dreamy features managed a small frown. "Vanilla thrill-ah? What on earth — ? Does that have something to do with Las Vegas, Nicky?"

"I guess you were out of the country at the time. It has something to do with the opposite of loving — fighting." His loosely curled fist made a mock feint to her chin. "Which we will never do."

"Never," Van said dubiously. "Especially if you don't call me Vanilla in public," she warned. "Nicholas?"

He didn't answer, or if he did, Van was suddenly too sleepy to hear it.

♣ Chapter Sixteen ♣

MIDNIGHT LOUIE EXAMINES
HIS SITUATION

I do not have to spell it out for anyone who has spent any time and money in Vegas whatsoever. They are good days indeed when a new establishment is prettying up to open and the dice always seem to be landing seven-up all along the Strip and Downtown.

Naturally the whole town is atwitter over the new Crystal Phoenix, given Mr. Nicky Fontana's dark-horse mystique among Vegas front-runners and the even more mysterious shenanigans of an architectural and managerial nature going on daily in the ex-Joshua Tree. Las Vegans love long odds.

The old place is crowded now with construction workers, mirror installers, crystal hangers, electrical engineers, and neon artists, who are the most unusual of the lot. Not much salvage is available anymore from the old days, but luckily there are many new pickings for the likes of Midnight Louie.

It is indeed a pleasure to spend one's time around and about the Crystal Phoenix during reconstruction. With Mr. Nicky Fontana and the lady with the Lake Mead eyes, all is sunshine and sure things, as I hear every day while making my discreet rounds.

"Oh, Nicky," says she. "Do take a quick look at these new plans to see if you approve!"

And Mr. Nicky Fontana, he drops whatever he is doing, which nowadays is likely to be analyzing budget projections on computer printouts rather than eyeing racing forms or overseeing the architects instead of racing around Vegas in his Vette with the T-tops down, so Mr. Nicky Fontana, he rushes over and says like this:

"Oh, yes, Van, what is it I can do for you? Or would you like to indulge in a small intermission while we ankle over to the Dunes for luncheon?"

I tell you, it is enough to make an old Vegas hand more than somewhat queasy, were he not a sentimental old Joe at heart. But behind all the sap and sugar there is still plenty of vinegar running or my moniker is not Midnight Louie, which it is since the time I am old enough to be admonished to exit my immediate surroundings in a hurry.

Now, it is known for a fact that although Miss Van von Rhine continues to inhabit the suite numbered seven-eleven, Mr. Nicky Fontana finds it necessary to visit her frequently for late-night emergency sessions, strictly having to do with hotel business, of course. Miss Van von Rhine's dainty high heels no longer make the journey up in Mr. Nicky Fontana's private elevator.

But this may be to squash uneducated talk, as it is also true that Mr. Nicky Fontana's ladyfriends suddenly are making themselves scarce, as is the esteemed Nostradamus and other Las Vegas landmarks.

Not hide nor one peroxided hair of the enchanting Miss Roxelle has been seen since her last appearance and sudden departure, and even Miss Darcy McGill, one of the handsomest hoofers to grace the Las Vegas boards, no longer requests to visit Mr. Nicky Fontana's rooftop whirlpool for the benefit of her physique, even though she is sometimes seen to limp on her outings to the hotel.

She is no one's fool, Miss Darcy McGill, and is known to consider this her greatest flaw in a city that sometimes seems to exist merely to reward folly, although no one can fault her gams.

Some may challenge the insights of a mere hanger-on such as myself into the intimate domestic arrangements of highfalutin folks like the honchos of a brand-new Vegas hostelry. But such shortsighted individuals overlook a lifetime's experience of getting around quietly, keeping my ears perked, my mouth shut, and my tail well out of the way of anyone's size thirteens.

I conclude it is plain that prime opportunity awaits an all-around handy guy like myself at the Crystal Phoenix. Although no one hears one syllable about who is behind the muscle trying to move in on Mr. Nicky Fontana, the three beach boys do not show up again, no doubt deterred by my vigilant presence, as well as frequent inspection visits from the brothers Fontana in full Family gear, which is to say packing sufficient iron to sink the QE Two and its lifeboats.

Even his uncle Mario comes by on occasion to pinch Mr. Nicky Fontana's cheek with proud affection and to attempt the same now and again with Miss Van von Rhine, only in an area where cheeks of quite another sort are to be found. But this is a seldom thing and Miss Van von Rhine is less liable to take offense these days.

So events are moving along in a spirit an optimist would call peachy-keen, and I am all set to put my professional services at the disposal of the Crystal Phoenix for good and all when the blond doll in the Charles Jourdan pumps sashays in with an eelskin briefcase one Monday morning and makes straight for Mr. Nicky Fontana's penthouse in the clear view of six carpetlayers, twelve mirror installers, one electrician, a vagrant who got mislaid with the carpeting, myself — and Miss Vanilla von Rhine. (Midnight Louie knows all.)

♣ Chapter Seventeen ♣

Van stared at the closed stainless-steel elevator doors, absently sticking a pencil behind her ear and letting her armful of architectural plans droop.

Beside her, a momentarily ignored Walter Maxwell, fedora in hand, was turning slowly under the newly installed ceiling to admire glittering swags of crystal ruffled like an Austrian sheer into a solid canopy of icy bright light.

"Not bad," he said. Van looked at him sharply, then back to the elevator doors. "The lights, I mean," Maxwell modified rapidly. "Quite impressive."

"How did she get a key?" Van asked, more puzzled than perturbed.

"The . . . uh, young lady?" Maxwell cleared his throat, a helpful stalling technique for lawyers caught flat-footed, and especially those who lived in Las Vegas. "Funny, I thought she was you when I first got here. I followed her in, in fact."

"Me?"

"She looks like you. From behind, I mean. Blond, and a certain classy way of walking —"

Van's face darkened on each blurted phrase, turning especially dire at the word "classy." But her voice remained cordial.

"Come to my office, Mr. Maxwell; I'll show you the rest of the plans for the Crystal Phoenix. You haven't seen anything yet!" Van von Rhine lifted a limp wave of soft blond hair from her forehead.

The final phrase, and the enthusiasm, reminded Maxwell

179

of Nicky Fontana, if the diction didn't.

"Nicky mentioned a roof of colored water too?"

"That's for the Crystal Promenade. I'm hoping the hotel gets some publicity on that; it's the first nonresidential application of the technique I know of."

Maxwell took in Van's plain but paper-swamped office with encouraging wonder. "I don't know how you did it, Miss von Rhine, but it looks like the Phoenix is going to come roaring right up from the ashes with a bang."

"Is that what they're calling it already — just the Phoenix?"

"A shame, since the whole moniker's so classy. But it's like Caesars, you know. Everybody and everything's gotta have a nickname in this town."

"What's yours?"

"Maxie."

Van extended an elegant hand. "Mine's . . . Vanilla. Have a chair, Maxie."

"Thanks, but —" Maxwell had lifted some tented architectural plans from the sole remaining chair to reveal an oversized black cat in the process of opening one baleful eye of unforgiving jade. He elected to remain standing. "You don't really want me to call you Vanilla; you'd take my head off."

"I haven't taken a head off since breakfast."

"Then maybe Nicky would," he added cautiously.

Van, or Vanilla, smiled sweetly. "Van will be fine. There's no need for formality between us, Maxie. You've been playing project matchmaker since the beginning. Why, if it weren't for you, this hotel would still be a . . . a paper phoenix." She rattled plans under his disavowing nose.

"Matchmaker? Me?" Maxwell blanched and clutched his hat to his stomach, which had been troubling him of late.

Maybe he hadn't come by the Crystal Phoenix often enough, but something had changed. For one thing, Vanilla . . . Van von Rhine's face was showing a wicked little dimple whose existence he'd had no earthly reason to suspect before.

"Is it true?" he blurted. "What they say? That you and Nicky are —" Description failed him, especially if it didn't come prefaced by ample "heretofore's" — and what he was thinking definitely didn't.

"Are what, Maxie?"

"Uh, making this a real partnership deal? I hear Nicky's told his uncle Mario that you are single-handedly turning the old hotel into the finest flophouse — I mean accommodations — west of New Orleans."

Van's quirking mouth screwed the dimple deeper than a beauty mark.

"We aim to accommodate at the Crystal Phoenix, Maxie. Say, that might make a good advertising motto, what do you think, Maxie? It rings with a certain Western informality."

"I can't say. I hail from Cincinnati. Um, all these plans look splendid, er, Van. Splendid. I'll stop in again soon, when I can. Say I said hello to Nicky."

"Hello, Nicky," Van echoed obediently, her face lighting up like the crystal ceiling. Maxwell caught his age-diminished breath and attempted to puff out his shallow chest under the defensive hat in high hopes. But she was looking beyond him . . . behind him.

"Hi, Maxie!"

And there was Nicky Fontana, holding up the doorframe and claiming his territory, as usual. He smiled at Van and thumped Maxwell heartily on the back as he passed him. Then he evicted the black cat with firm hands and sat in the chair. "How goes it?"

Coughing discreetly, Maxwell edged for the door. Miss von Rhine — Van — was right; the temperature was high in here, more so since Nicky Fontana had entered, creating a subliminal heat wave that seemed to require only two sources of sizzle.

"Fine. I'm fine," he assured them. "The hotel looks fine. And you both look . . . fine! 'Bye." He vanished behind the closing door.

Van burst out laughing.

"What did you do to the poor guy?" Nicky wondered.

"I asked him to call me Vanilla."

"Hey, that's my prerogative!"

"Only in private. Publicly, using the name might lend me a dash of Las Vegas flash."

Nicky leaned across the paper-piled desk, crushing stiff plans noisily, to cradle her chin in the fork of his hand.

"But then if we get married, you'll be Vanilla Fontana. It sounds like an ice-cream sundae."

"We haven't said anything about getting married." Her features had tightened to the old look. Nicky diagnosed it as cold feet overriding a hot heart.

He shrugged, leaned out of his chair to kiss her lips lightly, and lounged back among the crackling plans. "There are twenty-one wedding chapels in the naked town; who knows? We might get the irresistible urge to sample one."

"Now *that* sounds like Baskin-Robbins," retorted Van, changing the subject. "And besides," — an edge to her voice made Nicky look up sharply from consoling the displaced cat with rhythmic caresses — "you can't go anywhere now. You have company upstairs."

Nicky's hand slapped his forehead. "I forgot! The penthouse decorator awaits! I'm jazzing up the old joint. You did use the seven hundred and fifty thou down here?"

"No good hotel manager refuses money."

"Don't look so guilty; you're right. 'A penthouse is a status symbol for certain insecure guests whose egos need boosting.' Better the big dough be lavished on the paying customers."

"Where did you hear that penthouse line?" Van's face had whitened to the color of Chef Song's rice cakes.

"Max-ie." Nicky nodded and grinned at the closed door. "After all, he is the Family lawyer. He's gotta report disloyal talk." Standing, Nicky stretched his limber body as unselfconsciously as the mirroring feline uncoiling at his feet. "That's what I pay him for — snitching."

"And you pay me to think of things like . . . oh, what a waste of time and money penthouses are."

"Yeah. So I won't waste much dough on it, I promise." Nicky winked and ducked out the door.

"He will be the despair of me," Van told the cat in heightened exasperation. Her tones grew silken. "Did the mean man take your chair, pussums?"

But despite Van's attempt to restore it to its habitual seat, the cat eeled from her custody, unwilling to accept favors where it expected to rule.

Van, hands on hips, sighed at what amounted to the third defection from her office in as many minutes. For some reason, the figure of the mysterious blond visitor to Nicky's lodgings strode into her mind on efficient mid-height heels.

Impeccably groomed and refined, she had been as alike to Van as one die to another. Van frowned. She was the one who had insisted their relationship remain unconfining, the one who lightly eluded the chains of commitment and mention of marriage. Despite her distance, she could not evade the easy, old-shoe rightness of being together that was worth twenty crystal slippers to any woman.

So why had Nicky hired a virtual twin of Van to help him with the penthouse? And, worse, appeared not to notice the similarity? Was the woman "insurance" — easy compensation — if Van proved too skittish? Well, why not? They had sworn no vows, pledged no fidelities. Van no more owned Nicky than she owned his hotel. She was just, after all, hired help.

Her fist hit the desk, rustling the papers madly. Damn it, she'd put too much of herself into the Crystal Phoenix, into everything and everybody that had anything to do with the Crystal Phoenix, to let anyone stop her now — even "outside muscle" of the distinctly feminine variety.

"I got the scoop on 'Nicky's folly,' Van. I thought you should be the first to know."

Darcy McGill's pert dancer's face, neat as a cat's, peeped through Van's ajar office door a few days later.

"Oh! Hi, Darcy. What's he done now?"

Darcy tiptoed in dramatically, shut the door and collapsed on the chair, first scooping up the sleeping cat in her long arms. She cradled it expertly, rubbing her nose down its decidedly paunchy tummy.

"Oh, you are an old softie." She looked up at Van. "So am I. I couldn't help notice those harried looks you throw her highness when she comes mincing through the stardust and the glitter every day to visit the room at the top."

It hadn't taken long for everyone in the hotel — and some out of it, Van knew, to notice Nicky's new consultant and to suspect delinquency.

"Really, Darcy, I know you're an old friend of Nicky's, but that doesn't give you the right to —"

"You didn't know that's all I was at first, though — did

you, Van?" Darcy grinned and tickled the cat with fluid fingers. "You thought I was the competition."

Van stiffened. "This isn't a matter of 'competition.' "

"Sure it is, Van. Don't be silly, or worse, proud. Look, Nicky's always had lots of girlfriends. He did even in grade school. He's like this old shmoo here, aggravating but loveable.

"I wouldn't say anything, except this time it's different. This is man-woman stuff; it's serious. I'd hate to see the green flames of jealousy" — Darcy propped up the cat so its chartreuse eyes confronted Van — "ruin something great for two good friends of mine.

"So I snooped, figuring you'd die before asking Nicky. Her name's Arden Holloway; she's an interior decorator from the smart side of town, and other than bearing a less than casual resemblance to you in face, figure and manner, she seems to come here on purely professional errands. Nicky's really redecorating the penthouse on his own. I've checked the wallpaper orders to prove it."

"I never doubted it," Van began doubtfully.

"Hah! You may look like a cool customer, but under that marzipan exterior beats a heart of pure possessiveness! So relax. Nicky's being a good boy, I swear. Now you keep concentrating on the Taj Mahal here and stop worrying. I've got a va-va-voom dress to wear to the opening gala and nobody is going to stop me!"

Darcy flung the cat to the floor and her long body out of the chair and to the door in one smooth motion. There she posed in classic showgirl stance — hand on cocked hip, arm flung high, chin up, ankle prettily turned.

"You're a regular private eye, Darcy."

"Very private," Darcy said, winking one hazel peeper. "And very cheap."

★ ★ ★ ★ ★

"You're tense," Nicky observed.

Van sat on the edge of her bed, still dressed for dinner in an ivory silk pantsuit she'd bought at a shopping arcade boutique during a lunchtime trek.

Nicky's sure fingers massaged her temples, the bed creaking companionably as he rested one knee behind her.

"Making a hotel over is as tough as pulling payoffs out of Nostradamus," he mused in a voice smoother than fettuccine Alfredo. "It's a good thing I thought this project would be fun."

"You must be having fun redoing the penthouse," Van said suddenly.

The silken circling motion of Nicky's fingers stopped cold. "I have more fun doing this," he said. Suddenly he rolled backward on the bed, one arm hooking her midriff to sweep her atop him.

"Nicky, we'll ruin our good clothes," Van protested, more troubled by the inner specter of a ragged relationship than any outer déshabillé.

"So ruin 'em." Nicky, on his back, was engaged in arranging Van upon himself as if she were a pet cat.

"You're very distracting," she conceded.

"You deserve distraction." His fingers sought the silk of her skin beneath the loose garments. "Giving it's a tough job, but somebody's got to do it. And you get all the hard work —"

"But isn't it worth it?"

Caresses paused as they measured each other's eyes. That evening had marked the debut of the new marquee neon. Nicky and Van had celebrated by dining atop the Landmark Hotel tower for an unrivaled view of the Strip's nightly light show.

Waiting for the prearranged moment when the Crystal Phoenix marquee joined the fireworks, Nicky had held Van's hand across the snowy table linen. While they watched, a new ring of light exploded into life around the black obscurity of an otherwise dark building. It felt like attending the birth of a star.

Van's eyes had sprung tears, and Nicky's hand had nearly crushed hers within a fistlike grip.

"The best Strip-tease I ever saw," he joked. "Look, here comes the sign."

Not far from where the Flamingo Hilton's avarian showoffs flounced pink neon feathers, an ice-blue phoenix unfurled triumphant neon wings and sent magenta ripples running rings around the darkness under a cascade of pulsing white-water lights meant to represent a fountain.

"Someday soon those dark thirteen stories will be lit up like an electric chessboard," Nicky said in a high-voltage voice, leaning back into the Landmark's barrel-shaped lounge chair.

"Fourteen," Van corrected automatically. It was one issue she remained adamant upon.

Instead of answering, Nicky raised her hand and shifted his tight grip just enough to free her knuckles for the hungry brush of his lips.

A wordless, highly charged bond stretched between them, unlikely partners in a dream whose distant extravagance dazzled even its dreamers.

"It's gorgeous!" Nicky breathed as he watched through the windows, still holding her hand tight.

"That's what you always said it would be, even that first day."

"Did I? I must have been . . . obnoxious."

"Unremittingly. But you were right."

"I picked the right manager."

Van had stirred in her chair, the spell broken. Far away the lights melded into the speeding blur that rings in the riders on a carnival carousel.

She didn't feel like a "manager" when she and Nicky shared an emotional moment. She wished he wouldn't confuse the issue, that he could recognize their professional and personal associations as two different things, that their partnership was uneasily founded on reluctant mutual respect and undeniable attraction.

Now she lay in his arms in her hotel bedroom, still vaguely disturbed. Someday soon, she told herself, the hotel would be done. And so would this.

Nicky's searching mouth fastened on hers, but even as Van mentally catalogued her objections to the futility of passion without the promise of a future, he suddenly wrenched away.

He rolled off the opposite side of the bed and went to stand at the uncurtained window.

"What's the matter?" she asked.

"Your heart's not in it," he answered. "It's like trying to kiss the surf. Every time you're about to drown in your own tide, you ebb back all the way to China."

"How can you be so sure?" Van asked, miffed. He made her sound as mechanical as Hoover Dam.

He turned from the rectangle of night, the details of his form equally black against it.

"Because I love you, Van. That makes you easier to read than Nostradamus's pan when he owes me dough."

She sat up, cautiously. "Maybe love makes it easier to *mis*read people."

"Not me." He sounded very sure of himself. "Doesn't it

mean anything to you that I said I loved you? I don't do it every day."

"Oh, Nicky . . . you have been loved by everybody and everything since you were bounced on your uncle Mario's knee. It's sweet that you include me in this expansive company —"

"It's not 'sweet'!" The words exploded on a wave of raw feeling, washing over Van with a stinging intensity. "It's hell." Nicky jammed his hands into his pockets and circled Van, careful to keep a precise distance between them that only his voice penetrated.

"I don't say that stuff that often, Van. Yeah, you're right. I've had more than my share of love — sometimes so much, it damn near smothered me, and what could I do? They loved me. Is that what I'm doing now, Van? Smothering you?

"I get the feeling you want to keep me just so far away — maybe at the ends of your pretty, pale fingernails. I can feel your fingers brushing me, all the time, just the faintest touch. The brush-off. The arm's-length treatment." He paused in his restless circling. "That's not good enough. I'm not the arm's-length type."

"And if I am?"

He stood even stiller. "I'll have to put up with it, I guess. But I'm sorry for you."

Her voice came softly. "It's . . . more strain than we realize, seeing dreams come true. The hotel —"

"Damn the hotel," he broke in, but she went on.

"The work, the worry. The paranoia, knowing there are forces that wish one would fail, that might make one fail —"

" 'One' — hell! Me! Us! The Fontana Family. It's called muscle, Van, and it's ugly and real, and I can fight that. I can't fight the kind of muscle you use. You flex it like a pro. I think it's just not caring enough."

"Then maybe you won't have to love me anymore," she suggested quietly.

He thought it over. "No." Nicky went to the door. "No, that won't happen."

She followed him. "Nicky, I don't want to hurt you. You're the nicest . . ."

His laugh was rueful. " 'Nice' is not enough, babe. 'Not wanting to hurt' isn't good enough when your words are running the razor down my veins. *You're* not enough — have you ever said you loved anybody?"

"Of course I have!"

"I don't mean *did* you ever love anybody. Sure, you did. You loved Daddy until he died and probably a few kindly nannies and maybe some stray cat, but did you ever *say* it?"

"It's different for you!" At last her voice sawed cleanly through raw emotion. "It's easy for you! You belong to a clan, for God's sake, Nicky! Your grandmother leaves you money, your uncle would kill for you, your brothers will fight for you, your dozens of friends will never leave you lonely. It's so easy to love when you've *been* loved. It's so easy to say it when you take it for granted!"

Nicky's hands on her elbows swept her into the corner behind the door, into the darkest part of the room. Only his voice lit the shadows, white hot.

"You ever wonder what happened to my papa, Van? Or why uncle Mario is head of the Family when he was my papa's younger brother? Or why my mama lives in California, like my grandmama did before she died — why I lived and went to school there?

"Papa *died,* Van, just like yours. Maybe he was a warmer man than your father, maybe I loved him more than you loved yours — I don't know. But he's just as cold and dead now. He died in a restaurant. Over a plate of Mama

Tinucci-brand pasta. Lead poisoning's what they used to call it. The police called it a Gangland Killing.

"The killers sprayed the place with bullets and spaghetti sauce and blood. Papa pushed me under the table at the first shot. It was my birthday, see. That's why we were there. That's why they knew he would be there — all alone in Mama Tinucci's brand-new restaurant. With just me, no muscle."

Only the sound of Van's horrified sobs shattered the dark now, but Nicky didn't seem to hear them.

"That's why we went to California. I was twelve; my mama and grandmama said that they'd had enough of it, that I needed a . . . vacation from Fontanas. I didn't come back until after college, until after Mama Tinucci was gone, and then only because I had to." His voice made a wrenching attempt at lightness. "I guess you can take the boy out of Las Vegas, but you can't take Las Vegas out of the boy."

Shock had made Van breathless. "That's why . . . why your grandmother left you her money, why your family didn't want you to rebuild the Crystal Phoenix. That's why they all rallied around at the first sign of danger! They feel they must protect you after that."

"Yeah, but they can't." Nicky's voice had roughened again. "They can't protect me from you."

She put her hands to his shoulders, to the lapels of his silk-weave sport coat, almost expecting to feel a spaghetti slick on the immaculate fabric, to see bullets erupting in lava-red spumes from the dark, to smell powder and spaghetti sauce, and to touch fresh blood blossoming like a red carnation in his buttonhole.

Nicky spun her around again, pushing himself into the corner now and bringing her with him, pressing her to him as if they were two children hiding, so close, their ribs dovetailed.

Van felt herself sucked into the fierce maelstrom of his emotion, felt herself about to be siphoned into the still eye of his storm of love and pain.

"No," she protested to the unhearing elements that claimed her, the least of which was love. Nicky's hunger found her, took the "no" from her mouth, and replaced it with the life-affirming "yes" written on his lips.

Such a man would force a phoenix from the ashes, Van thought as Nicky's kiss consummated the union of their weaknesses as completely as their workaday alliance had united their separate strengths.

Dizzy, still swathed in the dim room's darkness and something even more tenebrous than that, Van pulled away for a determined moment.

And Nicky, quelled at last by the violent embrace he'd begun, read revulsion in her withdrawal. He apologized as best as he could, his voice almost inaudibly husky.

"I said before this wasn't my style. Maybe I was wrong."

She shrugged slightly under his hands, in a cold, heedless way that further chilled his cooling blood.

"Nicky . . ." Hands as soft as corn silk found his face. "I — I'm afraid I might . . . love you too."

Shock silenced them both. Neither moved, although their breathing came in tandem after a while. After an even longer while, she spoke again. "I'm sorry if that scares you. That's not my style."

"What is your style?"

"I don't know."

"Then let's find out."

"My father died of love," she told him later, much later, while they lay under the white firmament of sprayed-on plaster and watched faint rainbows of reflected neon dance like the aurora borealis over the ceiling.

"How?"

"In a hotel — like this but not like this. Behind a closed door that I wasn't supposed to notice. Doing something that little girls aren't supposed to know their elders do. Except I don't think it was love; it was necessity."

"Maybe you're wrong." Nicky's hands warmed her from the limpid dark. "Sometimes we underestimate our parents' capacity to love. Maybe he just couldn't show it."

"I don't know. I only know I don't want to be left out like that again, to be behind the door someone closes in my face —"

"Life is full of closed doors, Van, and closing doors. Nobody can protect you from that. Not even the censor in your soul."

She turned to him, the sheets rustling conspiratorily. "And nothing can guarantee that you will be taken seriously, Nicky. Not even the most vaulting of ambitions."

"Just you." Nicky's fingers tunneled into her hair to hold her face still. "Just you take me seriously, Vanilla mine. I mean what I say."

He put his face alongside hers and said what he meant. "I love you."

The words rose above the homely hum of the air conditioner. "Trust me."

♣ Chapter Eighteen ♣

"Good morning, Miss Holloway."

Van, surrounded by the chaos of her construction-debris-littered lobby, beamed like a summer sun on a seaful of flotsam, thereby enobling it.

The interior designer, who'd been making another of her brisk, almost furtive passages through the mess on her way to the penthouse elevator, paused.

"Lovely day, isn't it?" Van went on. "This trash will be cleared away soon. It's rather hard on expensive leather." She glanced at the woman's sawdust-veiled Jourdan pumps.

Miss Holloway's feet tapped impatience as she let the overstuffed eelskin briefcase sag to the end of her arm. Her other hand held a fat, vinyl-bound sample book by its built-in suitcase handle.

"I hope Mr. Fontana's renovation is going well," Van said, probing shamelessly.

"Very well," Miss Holloway said, beginning to turn, catching her calf with the corner of the sample book, gasping in pain and dropping the heavy case.

Van had crouched to retrieve it before the woman could. The covers lay splayed askew, wallpaper and fabric samples fanned in plain sight on the new navy-plush lobby carpeting.

The woman seemed eager to shovel the revealed pages out of sight, but inch-long artificial fingernails lacquered in delicate pink prevented much progress.

Van's own sensitive fingertips, the nails short and polished clear, ran over the exposed samples, over crewcut patterns of endless flocked velvets and slick gold foils, over the rough corks interspersed with gilt flakes as garish as fool's gold.

The woman's eyes met Van's through the cerise tint of her faceted resin sunglasses. She shoved them suddenly atop her sleek ash-blonde head.

"There's a lot of background to cover up there," Van noted.

"Yes. We're selecting wall and floor coverings first. Mr. Fontana is . . . most precise about what he wants."

"I'm not surprised," Van said, happy to observe that Miss Holloway's eyes were a nondescript gray shade. "This must be one of your more unique design assignments."

The woman stood, once again with a firm grip on her cases.

"Very unique." Humor winked from the murky gray eyes for the first time. "As unique, I think, as this hotel will be. In its own way, of course. Now, if you'll excuse me, Miss von Rhine —"

"Van." The woman arched her eyebrows at the unrequested intimacy, the only portion of her anatomy free to gesture. Van smiled. "Any friend of Nicky's is a friend of mine. I'll turn the key for you," she added, leading the way through the litter to the stainless steel elevator and producing her own key to unlock the doors.

"Thank you, Van," Arden Holloway limped onto the elevator with her gaudy burdens.

Van decided then and there that she absolutely needed and deserved the ninety-dollar silk scarf at Ultra Vegas that matched her eyes. She waited until the doors, shut again, presented a steely satin mirror image of her serene self — and Darcy McGill towering behind it.

"I told you she was no competition," Darcy said.

"No, and judging from the decorating samples I just saw, the penthouse decor will be no competition for the rest of the hotel. No wonder the poor woman's been slinking through here like a criminal! She has to cater to the innate Fontana taste." Van sighed. "Well, that's her problem, thank God."

"And yours. Unless Nicky finds another place to hang his satin pjs."

"When did you blow in?" Van asked, turning to change the subject.

"With the industrial vacuum cleaners. This lobby gets dirtier and noisier every day. Is it ever going to be done?"

"Soon, very soon."

Darcy grinned impishly and rattled the white bakery bags dangling from each fist. "Danish. Croissants. Jelly-centered doughnuts. I thought you could use a pig-out. And the crew, too."

"That's sweet of you, Darcy."

"Just saying thanks for the use of the whirlpool."

"You haven't used it lately."

Darcy lifted one meticulously plucked eyebrow. "No, and won't again. But past favors, you know. Where's Nicky today?"

"Assembling the in-house carpentry staff. It's taking some time to recruit carpenters who not only understand the fine points of gaming table construction, but can adapt to some of our innovations, like Ultrasuede-covered rim cushions instead of the usual vinyl."

"Ultrasuede! You kill me, Van! When Nicky ordered class, he got it with a capital 'C' — for Cash flow!"

Van only laughed and started stringing the sweet rolls along a temporary work counter that served as an informal snack stand when needed.

"Goodies courtesy of a friend of management," Van sang out to the busy workers scattered here and there through the vast lobby. "Stop by on your breaks!"

Darcy shook her head on her long, graceful dancer's neck. "This place doesn't even smell the way it used to. It's like trying to see Christmas presents still surrounded with torn wrappings, but I think you've got a winner here, Van."

"We hope. The hotel business is . . . iffy. I just pray nothing goes wrong before the opening next month."

"Hi, Darce." Nicky was hurrying over, trailing fabric swatches. "Van, the guys are real dubious about this Ultra-whatever stuff here. They say wet booze glasses'll ruin it."

"It's washable, and besides, we have the bar rail below it to hold drinks."

Nicky's face registered 7.8 on the doubt scale.

"Ooh, that's yummy." Darcy fingered the burgundy Ultrasuede. "I'd feel like a lucky loser to rest my fevered fingers on that stuff."

"And this is for the high-action tables, with minimums of over a hundred," Nicky volunteered, thrusting forward a napkin-sized sample of burgundy cordovan leather embossed with the gilt Crystal Phoenix medallion design.

"I better get out of here before I volunteer to be a change girl here or something," Darcy said with one last, lustful look at the fabrics. "Take it easy, friends. I want something left of you two by opening."

With joint assurances of that likelihood, Van and Nicky saw her off and stood studying the activity-filled lobby.

"Say, this phoenix leather stuff would be great on my Corvette seats," Nicky mused. "D'you suppose there'd be enough left over — could we afford it?"

Van smiled tolerantly. "I guess 'we' could afford it.

There isn't much to the seats in your Corvette. Oh, speaking of fine design," she added impishly, "your P.I.D. just slipped up to the penthouse."

"P.I.D.?"

"That woman I keep seeing."

"That's no woman." Nicky grinned triumphantly at Van's bemused expression. "That's my interior decorator."

"Are you sure that's all?"

A look of innocence swaddled Nicky's form like a blanket. "Hey, do I look like the type of guy who'd go for some blond with a bun on her head? And what's this P.I.D.?"

"Personal Interior Decorator."

"You knew who she was all the time — damn! I forgot she was coming." Nicky dumped the swatches onto the snack table and turned for the elevators. "If you see Nostradamus, tell him I'm too busy to bet — on anything!"

Van plucked a chocolate eclair from the makeshift smorgasbord and ambled back to her office. With the planning stages past, her job meant overseeing details now, answering endless questions and interviewing potential employees along with Nicky. It wasn't as much fun, but necessary.

A brother Fontana in a white Bogart suit, complete with everything but sweat stains, stepped from the shadows leading to her office.

"Anything wrong?" she asked.

"Nah, but uncle Mario wants us to keep an eye on things until the new security staff's on duty." He eyed the long pastry in Van's hand, which was the size of a small submarine and slathered with chocolate frosting.

"Want a bite?" she found herself offering. "Or can't you eat on duty?"

The young man — Ralph? Ernesto? Or someone unmet yet, like Giuseppe? she wondered — studied the object uncertainly.

"I don't want to get goo on my trigger finger — bad for the nickel plating, if you know what I mean, but I guess a bite wouldn't hurt."

Leaning forward, his wolf-wide jaws amputated the eclair's top third. A quick lick restored his face to a more credibly threatening condition; not one smudge of chocolate frosted the white suit.

"The Fontana gift for ingenuity never ceases to amaze me," Van remarked.

"May you never cease to never cease," he returned, resembling a guardian angel from a 1940s movie, and touched spotless fingers to the brim of his panama hat. "We've got to check in with a man from uncle. Be back soon."

Back in the office, Van found her favorite feline curled in his favorite chair.

"I could get used to brothers," she told it, sitting in her chair to eat what was left of her lunch.

The cat sat to attention with sleepy, owl-like gravity, winking first one emerald eye, then another. It stretched, bridging the chair from armrest to armrest, then thumped to the floor and thumped again atop her desk.

There its face wrinkled until its white whiskers twitched. It assumed an expression of such awful deprivation, its eyes weeping half-shut, that Van pinched a generous corner off the eclair and presented it on the palm of her hand.

The animal crouched instantly, picking at the pastry, thick cream filling and all, until it was gone.

"You know, kitty," Van told it with fond sternness, "you are an outrageous hedonist and as severe a trial to my patience as Nicky Fontana, but I guess I'm stuck with you — both."

The cat applied itself to rigorously cleaning its whiskers and avoiding comment.

The crystal phoenix itself arrived in time for Christmas.

Like a treetop angel, it descended on McCarran Airport from above. It came upon a midday clear, embedded in a rough but sturdy crate, marked Fragile in such graceful lettering that the word was obviously meant to be pronounced in the original French, France being the Phoenix's point of origin.

"Frah-jheel," Walter Maxwell muttered to himself as he escorted the crate back to the hotel in the cushy upholstery of his ice-blue limousine. Beside him, Nostradamus, silent for now, frantically plied his brain for a rhyme for "fra-gill-ee."

"Jeez, I'm snowed under up here, Van," Nicky complained when she rang the penthouse to tell him of the arrival. "I didn't know redecorating could be so much work. Look, I'll get down as soon as I can. In a minute."

So Van paced alone in the lobby, waiting for the centerpiece of the Crystal Phoenix to sink to rest upon its appointed nest.

A circle of rich navy carpeting, duly stamped with the gold phoenix signature medallion, had been vacuumed to pristine plushness. A custom Plexiglas pillar eighteen inches in diameter marked the lobby's center, gleaming like a plinth of polar ice, its empty top surface bald of its crowning glory.

Two glaziers toted in the crate while Maxie and a kibitzing Nostradamus trailed them like nervous courtiers. The bookie was muttering rhymes like prayers.

"I haven't been so edgy since Ali fought Frazier. My

money's on the crystal, but not on the glazier."

At that instant one of the glaziers stepped on a piece of unclaimed pipe and slipped. Workmen froze. Van clutched her heart, or where she thought it should be, and found not even a feeble blip.

The glazier caught himself, hurled himself forward a few fast steps, his fellow toter stumbling with him, then straightened and moved on to sighs of relief so universal that it sounded as if the sea had invaded Las Vegas.

Near the pedestal the workmen stopped, drawing screwdrivers from their hip-slung tool holsters to disassemble the crate. Clumsy wooden sides were gently lowered. Van hovered near to watch the inner packaging peeled away.

At last it stood under the myriad crystal droplets of the ceiling, catching light, shattering it, dashing it to smithereens on the reflective surfaces all around — the crystal phoenix Van had commissioned from the great French glass house of Lalique.

It was magnificent — sheer winged ice rising from the glassmaker's fires, a thing of clarity and crystalline perfection — legend personified. Van stared at it, remembering the late-working evening Nicky had found and frowned over the bill.

"Forty grand? For a glass knickknack? This Lalique joint has taken you to the cleaners —"

She had hushed him with a quick kiss. "It's 'Lah-leek,' darling, not 'Lall-i-cue.' And pieces like this are commissioned as gifts to kings, queens, and popes. Maybe you're right, though. Maybe it's too good for the Crystal Phoenix."

"Hey!" The bill was swiftly turned over to make way for the next. "Nothing's too good for a class act like the CP. Or me," he said, getting down to some oddly appropriate billing and cooing instead of mere bill-reviewing, the phoenix forgotten.

Now the bird stood here, caged in glass, its great unfurled wings skeining the air for slivers of silver light. The glaziers, hands gloved in flannel, lifted it atop its pedestal.

A hushed clapping sounded from all the happenstance occupants of the lobby, from friends and workers who had stopped to watch the installation ceremony.

Van felt she stood at an operatic ovation; her tears added yet another crystalline veil to see the world's light through. She wished Nicky were here, that he had made it down in time, and then, suddenly, she was glad he hadn't.

A shattering of glass rang out of tune, like wind chimes too suddenly stilled. Another burst of shattered glass struck their ears.

And another.

Applause ended as spontaneously as it had begun. The impromptu audience stood as frozen as the phoenix, staring at the fragile artwork, puzzled to find it yet poised on its pillar of light-iced Plexiglas.

Their ears located the crashing glass before their eyes could — the smashing sounds came from behind them, from the huge lobby's fringes.

A man in denim coveralls, his bare arms and chest muscle-knotted, kicked a wooden box from his path as he came forward. Shattered glass jingled as loud as payoff coins in a slot machine drop. He carried another box like a babe in arms. He stopped and dropped his arms. The box hit carpeting, the impact muted but its contents chiming brittle news of their destruction.

"Stop that!" Van instinctively stepped in front of the phoenix.

Another workman advanced, his hand heavy with a tool.

He passed under a twelve-foot aluminum ladder, then shoved it behind him like a door that needed closing. It toppled with a hollow crash. The man paused, lifted his implement to the ceiling. Crystals shattered to the pumping sound of explosion after explosion as bullets spat into their glittering midst.

The onlookers drew back.

More men were advancing — workmen by their dress, thugs by their vocations. Van recognized three hard faces from the night she had found strangers confronting Nicky in her office.

There were six men now, planted here to do battle at just this psychologically destructive moment. Here to destroy.

One spoke. "Too bad Nicky Fontana isn't here. It's like a Fontana to let a woman take his punishment for him. Tell Nicky Fontana that some of us object to turning a nice deserted place like the Joshua Tree into a junky Christmas tree.

"Tell Nicky Fontana if he don't get out of this hotel, we'll put out *his* lights next time. Tell him, but wait until we're done first, sister, and watch out for falling glass — !"

They brandished crowbars, pipes and huge crescent wrenches. One still carried a gun; Van guessed it had emptied itself on the ceiling. They came in a line, moving right through the central scaffolding unit beneath the main chandelier.

That was like walking under a ladder of sorts, Van told herself. Maybe it meant that their luck had a short fuse.

"Get outa the way, honey, and we'll clip the wings on that pretty glass bird of yours first, before we get around to the rest of it."

"No."

They paused in sheer surprise.

"This is *my* hotel." Her voice was crystal-cold. "I redesigned it. I worked on it until I couldn't see straight. I planned for every bar of soap in every guest room. I'm not going to make it easy for you."

"We don't have to make it easy for you either, honey." Another man spoke, his lips wore the same curl of uncaring scorn as the rest. "You get in our way —"

"I *am* in your way," she thundered back. "People like me have always been in the way of people like you — barbarians who'll take the shortest way to what they want."

"Callin' us names won't stop us. We want the bird and a lot more. You won't stop us, not a puny thing like you, and Nicky Fontana won't stop us and nobody around here won't stop us —"

Something stopped him, or his words at least — a fearful yowling in the distance, followed by enough clatter to announce the arrival of knightly horsemen.

Everyone in the lobby turned toward the hallway leading to the kitchen. A low black form shot from the tunnel of hall like a cannonball, something small and gold flapping at its forefront.

It drove straight for Van, as if it singled out her alone in all the confusion. It dashed in front of the line of thugs and sheltered at her ankles. A mouth yawned pink to spit a puddle of gold onto the freshly vacuumed carpeting. The glittering thing bucked indignantly, revealing itself to be a goldfish — an Acapulco Gold carp from Chef Song's private stock, to be precise.

Fast behind the fleeing cat came Chef Song himself in full Chinese battle cry, meat cleaver glinting. Behind him came Madame Song, armed with a cast-iron frying pan. Behind her came the dynasty Song, small but agitated and equipped with whatever their quick hands could curl around, ranging from butcher knives to egg-white whisks.

The family Song drew to a halt, en masse, and studied the situation, impeccably diagnosing the nature of what they had so headstrongly interrupted. Assorted Songs drew into a phalanx behind their grim parents, behind Van and the crystal phoenix.

Six pair of size-thirteen Hush Puppies shuffled on the soft carpet. Lengths of pipe and board and crowbar shifted from hand to hand.

"You're not going to stop us," the leader asserted a trifle sullenly. "Not for all the tea in China."

"But —" Van pointed out quickly. This time the men hung on every word. "The black cat just walked in front of you. Well, ran. That's very bad luck."

"It ran past you, too!" one man accused, flexing his biceps.

"But you were in its direct path. I was a mere bystander."

"I'm not gonna argue with you, lady, except to say you'll be more than a bystander now." The leader advanced, crowbar cocked. "You'll be mincemeat."

"If it's mincemeat you want, try over here," came a dry, familiar voice. Van glanced over her shoulder to see that Nostradamus had taken a position beside the Songs. His everpresent racing form hung folded like a hankie over something in his hand that made it crease in a remarkably straight line. "I won't leave enough of you guys to fill a flea's ear."

Beside Nostradamus stood Walter Maxwell, his hat pushed far back on his head, armed only by his baldness and the grimness of his face.

At the far-flung edges of the lobby, workers shuffled off a pall of self-interest, picked up hammers and screwdrivers and came slowly forward, ringing in the people gathered around the phoenix.

Van looked over her shoulder. It seemed a crowd stood behind her, friends and strangers, including the faces of the nondescript men who had staked out a claim on the lobby of the Crystal Phoenix long before it had held a future, but only a past.

She even thought she glimpsed a tall, silver-haired figure at the back, but she didn't dare keep her attention off the men in front of her. When she glanced back at them, their faces looked even more stupid with surprise. They hefted their makeshift weapons, but with no heart.

"Tell Nicky Fontana —" the leader began.

"Tell him yourself," came a voice from behind everybody.

Nicky stepped out of the elevator. The doors stayed wide open, as if they'd been set that way, as if they'd been that way for a while. He held a gun but didn't even bother to aim it.

"She's right," he told the thugs as he joined Van in front of the crystal phoenix. "It's her hotel. And their hotel." He waved at the people gathered behind them. "And their hotel." Nicky indicated the glowering workmen. "Everybody's worked too damn hard to let a bunch of snotty-nosed hoods too dumb to arm themselves properly wreck so much as a light bulb in this place.

"So you boys better climb that unlucky ladder you walked under and screw in the new bulbs the workers here will pass up. Your aim was lousy. You hardly broke any Austrian crystal pendants — we can order new ones in no time. Then you'll leave. And if you ever come back — in any shape or form — the new security force'll chop you up and feed you to the sushi chef. Got it? Then up that scaffolding, pronto!"

Nicky smiled modestly as applause burst out for a second time.

"Back to work," he threatened. "It may be your hotel, but I'm boss." He caught Van around the waist. "So's she." He leaned near to whisper. "You want to be security chief, baby? I can use a man like you. But you gotta wear Bermuda shorts, like those jungle johnnys, so the clientele can see your legs."

Van stopped him with a genteel kick in the shins undetectable to the casual observer, then turned to make sure the phoenix still stood unharmed.

"Quick, can you glaziers bolt on the Plexiglas cover before I have a heart attack?" She stepped back to let them work.

"You know what really scared me, Nicky?" she whispered. "I thought I saw the silver-haired man from upstairs lining up on my side! It was eerie."

He hugged her, laughed. "Ghosts, Vanilla baby, make good allies so long as you *don't* believe in 'em. I tell you, he doesn't exist."

She didn't argue, but watched from the safety of his arms as a secure transparent plastic box swallowed the crystal phoenix.

"Isn't it gorgeous, Nicky? The best thing you ever saw?"

"Not quite," he said under his breath. "And it isn't worth getting made into chopped liver for, either. But it *is* worth forty grand. So I guess it *is* an endangered species."

An explosion of an oath-like nature, in Chinese, distracted them from pursuing an embarrassing course of public nuzzling.

At their feet, to which Chef Song's trembling meat cleaver pointed eloquently, the black cat burped. Between its dapper black paws lay a damp spot containing no trace whatsoever — not so much as a scale — of a purloined goldfish.

♣ Chapter Nineteen ♣

MIDNIGHT LOUIE MUSES ON HIS FUTURE

Little does anyone present at what is soon to be known as "Von Rhine's Express," or "The Crystal Standoff" know the prime role that I, Midnight Louie, played in the entire denouement. (This denouement is a word of foreign extraction, namely French, and means the way things wind down.)

Although I do not make a big fuss about it, it is I who am instrumental in rallying the *habituées* (another French word) of the Joshua Tree, aka the Crystal Phoenix, to Miss Van von Rhine's defense, although she is doing a pretty good job of it on her own.

Naturally, one might think that Mr. Nicky Fontana is more than somewhat grateful for my guardianship of this little doll who is so obviously dear to his heart, but he has a lot on his mind these days and makes no overt gesture of bonhomie. (Another French tongue twister. You can see that by now I am immersed in culture of the first water and there is no choice but to make myself a key member of the Crystal Phoenix team.)

But first I must wait for the joint to open. And there is much work yet to be done, as Miss Van von Rhine is ever ready to remind Mr. Nicky Fontana when he is prone to get amorous in the office, which is most of the time.

Now, Macho Mario Fontana, he looks dimly on the idea of hoods running rife in the lobby of his nephew's new hotel — unless they are his hoods, of course, of which he wants to put

The Cat and the King of Clubs

a baker's dozen into place immediately. (He is most miffed that his litter of nephews had been lured away from the scene of the crime-to-be by a phony attempted theft of Mr. Nicky Fontana's Corvette in the parking lot. If you cannot rely on blood relatives in his line of work, who can you rely on?)

Miss Van von Rhine does not cotton to the idea, so Macho Mario comes up with the scam of slipping his boys into uniform as a security force, which is quite a switch for them. Luckily Miss Van von Rhine knows little of Las Vegas security forces and thinks that it is natural for such as they to pick their teeth with the tips of their jackknives and pursue other such habits as are common to hoodlums in the United States of America.

So although no one knows why such rabble as the bad boys who dropped in at the Phoenix would wish to throw their weight around in such a fine establishment, it does not cause anyone to lose much shut-eye, particularly Miss Van von Rhine and Mr. Nicky Fontana, who were not getting much sleep anyway, for reasons having no more to do with the hotel business than luck has to do with blackjack.

I, of course, expect to be handsomely rewarded for my services to the hotel, but do not press my claims upon the management, preferring to wait until the big opening bash and when everybody is in a good mood.

With my usual perception, however, I notice that some small concern seems to be making Miss Van von Rhine a bit down in the dumps lately — or should I amend that more than somewhat gauche expression to something a bit more uptown? Let us just say that Miss Van von Rhine is seen — to the observant eye, and my eye is nothing if not observant — to be a *soupçon triste*. That means a bit blue in the old pan more than somewhat.

(Ah, Louie, you are on a roll, *mon ami* . . . .)

♣ Chapter Twenty ♣

Rich burgundy carpet clung to the driveway curves like a velvet bodysuit. Long-stemmed silver champagne stands holding canna lilies stood floral guard on either side of the black-glass entry doors. Arc lights restlessly probed the sky above the Crystal Phoenix while the hotel, draped in as many light bulbs as a movie goddess's wardrobe has sequins, put on the ritz for its opening.

Everyone was invited and everyone came. Media, Beautiful People, tourists, high rollers from the East, low rollers from the budget tours of West Los Angeles, local beauties, beggars, bookies, and a visiting Arab pasha or two.

Outside, assorted junior Songs, attired in navy satin pajamas with burgundy piping, whisked visiting Mercedes, Rolls and an excessive number of Italian sports cars with unpronounceable names to parking lots.

Inside, the Leopard Lady, a Las Vegas regular notable for the invariably feline patterns of her wearing apparel (even her sunglasses were leopard-spotted in a 1960s harlequin shape that punk rockers often tried to roll her for), picked her way along the sinuous buffet table, collecting tomorrow's meals in her various shopping bags.

Gentlemen wearing light suits with dark shirts and white ties prowled unhampered. Ladies and gentlemen wearing the smart navy security uniforms of the Crystal Phoenix discreetly kept eyes and walkie-talkie ears on the aforesaid gentlemen.

Guests in every degree of dress ranging from fringe-and-rhinestone Western to black tie milled around the computerized carousels of video poker and pumped courtesy coins into the greedy guts of spanking new slot machines.

Carnival-colored chips slid rapidly across green felt, exchanging hands from house to guest and more often vice versa, at tables strung along the long crystal-lit casinos. Gold-capped fingernails as long as their owners' fashionably dangling ear cuffs tapped impatiently on soft Ultrasuede rim cushions while cards or dice fell into disfavor.

Along Slot-machine Row, abandoned lowball glasses kept company with empty paper cups bearing the hotel's phoenix emblem in gold on burgundy. Similar paper cups, overflowing with coins, slid across the pink-marble surface of the change booths and into relentlessly efficient machines that swallowed them en masse and then burped out an instant and accurate accounting.

New twenty-, fifty-, and hundred-dollar bills slipped into the hands of lucky winners. Losers slipped fresh fives, tens, and dollar bills under the metal grill in exchange for smaller coinage and hopefully better luck.

Around the crystal phoenix sculpture itself, center stage opposite the entry doors, gathered a motley assemblage.

The nine Fontana boys wore angelic off-white from toe to tie. Mama Fontana, in town for the occasion, accessorized a California tan with aqua charmeuse evening pants and a gold crocheted top. She was tall, enviably slim, and not at all what anyone who had not met her expected.

Uncle Mario seemed subdued in undertaker's black, with one red carnation impaling his lapel. Walter Maxwell, surprisingly, wore black tie and looked morosely self-satisfied. Nostradamus had produced a pin-striped suit of vague vintage. In its buttonhole bloomed a yellow canna lily, suspiciously reminiscent of the variety displayed in bunches outside the front doors.

Head and shoulders above the rest, even the men, stood Darcy McGill. What a dancer who regularly revealed nine-tenths of her epidermis on stage considered "va-va-va-voom" for social occasions turned out to be a floor-length plinth of Prom Pink crepe with chiffon bishop sleeves to her wrists and a monkishly draped cowl neck.

Van, nervous as a bride, tried to keep her hands off the sides of her white satin gown, which began with a strappy halter top entwined with pearls and flared to a trumpet skirt at the floor.

Her hair, for once, was not twisted up but allowed to duplicate the shining lines of her gown by fanning to her shoulders. At her wrist, because there was no possible perch for anything on her skimpy gown, bloomed a corsage of ruby-red roses interspersed with sprays of fragile lilies of the valley, a gift from Nicky Fontana.

Nicky himself was nowhere to be seen, having been summoned to attend to twenty major undisclosed crises occurring simultaneously offscene.

"Do you think it's going well?" Van asked for the thirteenth time, turning to the nearest available ear.

The ear was homely in the extreme but grew on a sympathetic face.

"I'll lay ten to one for a lobster dinner; this little joint's gonna be a big winner."

Nostradamus beamed just in time for the photographer from the *Las Vegas Review-Journal* to shoot Van and the bookie in unlikely camaraderie.

"Your name, sir?" the ignorant photographer barked, notepad in hand. He knew who Van von Rhine was, having already taken a formal shot of her and "hotelier" Nicky Fontana under the feverishly blinking phoenix marquee outside.

"Egbert," Nostradamus said meticulously. "E-g-b-e-r-t. Teague. T-e-a-g-u-e."

The photographer dutifully noted it.

Van stared at them both.

Nostradamus winked.

At their feet, something shifted. The black cat, now formally the hotel mascot and so pictured with Van in the Crystal Promenade for a Sunday feature story, wove through their legs, imparting static to Van's gown and thus encouraging the satin to cling even more than it inclined to.

"Nicky wants you."

Van jumped. Behind her towered the sedate Darcy, her face so deliberately blank it looked on loan from a Saturday night poker player.

"He called from the penthouse, Van. Something's up, I guess. Anyway, he said he needed you upstairs."

Van froze guiltily. "Oh, no . . . I hope he didn't blunder into — it's supposed to be a surprise!"

Darcy shrugged modestly draped shoulders. "Maybe he's got one for you."

Van was already racing for the house phones and then the elevator, wondering if she'd have to get the key. But the steel doors were wide and waiting. She pushed the button labeled "thirteen," shuddering slightly. Another last minute detail left undone. More remained. She and Nicky had their hands full. And if he'd stumbled onto the real surprise already. . . .

At the top, the doors split open on Nicky, looking like Prince Charming. He wore black, satin-striped trousers and a deep blue dinner jacket over a white ruffle-fronted formal shirt. Van wondered wildly if St. Jude's good will could broadcast through all that starch, and if they still needed it.

"Did you call me? Something you wanted to show me?"

"Yeah." Nicky's hand glided to her back to guide her along the hall.

Van planted high white satin heels. "Let's not play games. If you found it, you found it. Come on, I'll show *you*."

Nicky raised one jet-black eyebrow as Van brushed by him. Instead of entering the penthouse, she strode along the hall to the door cut through to the roof's remodeled guest whirlpool area.

The scaffold-mounted sheet plastic that separated Nicky's deck from the public area flapped in the soft night breeze. Below them, prime-time Vegas glittered, a rhinestone spiderweb. At their left, thrusting into the night like the prow of a dark crystal ship, rose a turret of tinted glass and steel.

"I called the electrician before I came up," Van said. "At least the lighting's fully functional. The rest isn't quite done. Wait a minute," she advised. "It'll come on in a second."

Nicky obediently stared at the alien construction. "What the hell is this?"

"It's where your extra seven hundred and fifty thousand dollars went, Nicky. It's — there, here come the lights!"

Around the turret's circular top two strips of rippling neon illuminated a Times-Square-style header. Then came the news broadcast to anyone with eyes in Vegas: Nicky Fontana's Crystal Carousel Club Now Open. Each letter scintillated like gold dust.

"You said, 'Surprise me,' " Van observed into the silence. "And I did take your name off the hotel." She held her breath.

He watched the illuminated letters circle round and round for perhaps three cycles, then cleared his throat.

"Um, isn't this a teensy bit . . . flashy?" Nicky asked delicately.

She turned to him, mouth agape in outrage — it was what he had been waiting for. He captured her lips in a kiss of the distinctly flashy variety.

"It's gorgeous, Van," Nicky approved happily when they finally separated to catch their breath.

"It's got a great view of the lights," she said eagerly. "It's totally see-through, three hundred and sixty degrees of view, except the glass is smoked. We'll book the finest lounge acts, aimed at an intimate audience, of course. It'll be the classiest nightclub in Vegas, you just watch, Nicky!"

"Vanilla, baby, you don't have to sell it to me. How'd you manage to slip it past me?"

"I put a public elevator through opposite your penthouse. You thought they were simply working on the expanded whirlpool deck for the guests. . . ."

"Oh, yeah, this." Nicky took her hand and led her down redwood steps past secluded spas bubbling solitarily into the night. "I approve. I approve of everything you do," he added, looking back through half-mast lashes. "Now I've got a surprise for *you*."

He was leading her back to the penthouse. Van balked again, this time before the plastic-covered scaffolding.

"Nicky, it's unlucky to go under there. Maybe another time." Her fingers twisted in his.

"Now," he insisted. "What are you afraid of?" His eyes were too direct to evade.

"Nothing!" she said quickly, her face white as her gown.

Nicky drew aside the wind-battered plastic and escorted Van under the scaffolding, then led her past his own vacant whirlpool to the glass doors.

"Nicky, I . . . I have to be honest." Glimpses of purple

flocked wallpaper and varicose-veined mirror tiles collided in Van's brain.

"Of course you do," he soothed. "Don't be nervous, Vanilla. This is one closed door you'll be glad you opened."

He swept back the sliding glass door, then turned to shut it, encasing them in silence and moonlit dusk. "Close your eyes," he invited in a tone so silken, she couldn't refuse.

Van's eyes squeezed shut. She heard Nicky's clothes rustle away and the click of a switch, then felt bright light dancing on her lids. Her eyes winced further shut.

"Open them." Nicky's arm tightened around her waist. She gripped his forearm with both hands. She didn't care if he lived in surroundings as garish as Liberace's museum on Tropicana Street, she told herself fiercely. If only she could hide her reaction to his ghastly decor. . . .

"Open them." It was an order now, and she did.

Van looked left, then right. Her mouth opened to match her eyes. She looked up, then down. She looked at Nicky, then back at the room.

"We're in the . . . bedroom."

"I moved the master bedroom down next to the living room. Who needs to waste time climbing all those spiral stairs? Now the secondary office and library is up there, with the game room. Guess who gets which one?"

"I . . . I can't guess anything." Van moved away from him, sinking into wall-to-wall cream-colored wool carpeting. She had expected a king-size bed and it was there, covered in muted Porthault bed linens. An ivory lacquer headboard and dresser furnished the room; smoke-glassed mirror discreetly dominated one wall. Even the walls were soft. She touched the creamy surface and felt ivory leather.

"You had the entire place redone — like this?"

"I had a little help." Nicky grinned. "From some snooty

interior designer who knew about these things. Someone likely to have insight into how a first-class blond with a bun would like things done."

"But the flocked wallpapers and the phony corks, the ghastly veined mirror squares in those boxes the hoodlums broke!"

"Decoys," Nicky admitted smugly. "I knew you'd peek. This here's the real McCoy."

"For me? You did all this — for me?"

He turned her to face the mirror, then wrapped his arms around her so tightly, she felt like white satin wallpaper plastered to his body.

"For us." Nicky nuzzled her neck. "To live in and to run the hotel from and be" — this part scared him, Nicky thought with sudden panic, but if ugly thugs with trunk-size biceps couldn't stop him, neither could dainty little dolls with impeccable taste — "and to be married in."

"Be married in?"

"Well, we'll get married someplace else — but to live in after we're married, which ought to be damn soon. Unless you don't like it." His forehead corrugated anxiously. "Unless it's not . . . classy enough."

Van squirmed around to face him.

"Nicky, I'd live in Liberace's limousine to be with you! This, this is first class! Posh to the portholes. But —" She pulled away mid-embrace and ambled to the bed, trailing the fragile scent of lily-of-the-valley. Her fingertips skimmed the luxurious linen. "I might . . . miss . . . some of your more decadent old flashy comforts a teensy bit."

Nicky grinned his triumph in a tackily open manner. "Hit those buttons on the headboard console, Vanilla baby."

Walking under the scaffolding had been lucky after all. She'd hit pay dirt on her first try. The ceiling over the bed peeled back with a discreet mechanical hum. Van looked up to see herself looking down.

"Hit it again, Van."

She did. The dusky mirrors slid away to reveal the midnight celestial floor show as the night's featured stars paraded in the skies over Las Vegas. Then everything slid away, and Van was enfolded in Nicky's arms for the first of what promised to be a series of absolutely top-drawer close encounters of the soon-to-be-marital kind.

♣ Chapter Twenty-one ♣

Epilogue, or MIDNIGHT LOUIE HAS THE LAST WORD

Stories such as this usually end with ". . . and so they get married and live happily ever after."

I like a happy ending as much as the next guy, and I would not be laying out the full skinny were I not to point out that Las Vegas is full of unhappy endings.

But for the Prince and the Princess, things turn out with a modicum of bliss. They get hitched in the Crystal Promenade at the biggest bash this town has ever seen, except for the opening of the Crystal Phoenix a month previous. Every limo in Vegas is present, with the exception of those belonging to shady characters who might wish the Crystal Phoenix ill.

Miss Darcy McGill is maid of honor, and if you think Miss Vanilla von Rhine makes a nice-looking little doll in her street clothes, you should eyeball her in seventy yards of imported Spanish lace on Macho Mario Fontana's arm as they come down the aisle. Macho Mario seems reluctant to give the bride away, but overcomes the temptation.

Mr. Nicky Fontana, of course, is the cat's pajamas in his tails. Nostradamus is best man and all the Fontana boys are ushers. Luckily, the littlest Song is female and gets to be flower girl. She carries this basket of lilies of the valley, which Mr. Nicky Fontana insists on, as he insists on lilies of the valley everywhere so the whole place smells like a flower factory.

You may detect a certain notable absence among the official bridal party, namely myself. Well, the truth is — and when do I tell you anything but the truth, the whole truth, and nothing but the truth? — the truth is that I am already on duty patrolling the grounds in my new capacity as undercover house dick for the Crystal Phoenix, the grandest little hotel to hit the Las Vegas Strip.

In fact, while everyone is watching the guests attempt to turn the former Miss Vanilla von Rhine into rice pudding and the current Mr. Nicky Fontana is attempting to whisk her away to an undisclosed honeymoon location, I am taking a small recreational dip in the hotel carp pond out back, unobserved except for a few pigeons flapping overhead and squealing their miserable lungs out.

Luckily, this does not interfere with the enjoyable tidbit I bestow upon myself as a reward for a job well done.

Unluckily, I am interrupted by Nostradamus, who slips away from the bridal festivities to smoke a stogie in the courtyard and discerns me in the act of disposing of a tail fin.

He comes over and leans down to blow a cloud of blue smoke directly in my kisser whiskers. I sense one of his more repellent bits of doggerel coming on. Nostradamus and I go way back.

"Well, who do I find with his paw in the pail, but Midnight Louie at the end of this tale."

With which feeble witticism he gives my posterior appendage an undignified yank. I do nothing but look up at the little bookie and give him a wink with one baby-green peeper.

After all, nobody in his right mind is going to squeal on a swell fellow like yours truly, who was born with his eyes shut and his mouth open but learns the hard way to do just the opposite and keep his eyes open and his mouth shut — and who intends to keep it that way for a good, long time.

♣ Tailpiece ♣

A Dialogue between Co-conspirators

I am shocked, appalled, and indignant. You say you have restored all of my cut lines, but I have a very skimpy part in the preceding proceedings, compared to my role in my current mystery outings.

Louie, your first books were written almost fifteen years ago. In the romance field then, just having you narrate was a bold step. The rule was that setting and secondary characters mustn't distract from the romantic relationship. So I had to keep you pretty low-profile.

It seems to me that I am portrayed as a rather fat and sassy dude, and I know that you cut the word "fluffy" from my first physical description.

Guilty as charged. You had longer hair in your first incarnation. I happen to like long-haired cats. When you moved from romance-mystery to mystery proper and you became a coverboy, your image was pumped up to the buzz-cut muscular silhouette on the Midnight Louie mystery covers today.

Call me Jean Claude. And you sometimes refer to me as an "alphacat." No doubt a tribute to my macho mystery reputation.

"Sam Spade with hairballs" is how I put it. True, you typify the hard-boiled, hairy-chested, mean-street walker who can't be bought and who considers himself catnip for the ladies. However, when I call you an "alphacat," I'm referring to the fact that — after *Catnap* and *Pussyfoot*, when your book titles went to the "cat and a color" title format beginning with *Cat on a Blue Monday* — they continue with an internal alphabet from "B" on.

Hey! I got toes and can count. That means, because you started with "B" on the third book, I will go Sue Grafton's famous "A is for" series one better. Let us hear it for feline power!

You will hear it for feline power when you make the money that Sue Grafton makes.

Spoilsport. Another thing that has always bothered me: why can I never speak in contractions, unless somebody-I-know's editing slips up?

That's because much of your "voice" is inspired by Damon Runyon, who wrote charming stories about the would-be genteel denizens of Broadway during the Depression, the bookies and con people, chorus girls and gamblers. That's where the "dolls" and "dudes" and other expressions come from, and why modern day Las Vegas is the best setting for you and your friends.

And I thought that *I* invented me! But, fess up, partner. You didn't do a thing when it came to creating the smooth dude that I am today. I am the genuine article, so to speak!

Yes, Louie, you are. Your name was spelled a bit differently, but the original "you" did live on stolen goldfish at a California motel. Your prototype was saved from Death Row at the local animal pound by a soft-hearted Minnesotan who flew you back to St. Paul, where I was a feature writer/reporter for the daily newspaper. You were not the smooth dude you are today: you attempted an inappropriate relationship with the woman's fixed female Siamese, and you refused to patronize the litter box for anything but digging expeditions. You were friendly enough to people, but you considered the Hoover vacuum cleaner and the lady's lawyer husband mortal enemies. So you ended up in a forty-dollar, three-inch entry in the classified "Pets" column, in search of the right home for a dollar bill. The ad intrigued me to write a feature story; you were such a fascinating subject that I let you put your saga in your own words.

A star is born! But I did not get a chance to speak again until you resurrected me for this Las Vegas Quartet twelve years later. What took you so long?

I didn't leave journalism to write fiction full time until eleven years after we met. I created the Las Vegas Quartet within a year of that, but it was shelved for almost five years, remember.

I hear you refer to our first editor on these books as "Lizzie Borden?"

Well, she took her editorial axe and slashed your lines by forty percent, and when the job was over and done, she slashed the rest of the manuscripts by forty-one.

Catchy phrase. How does this version of the book differ from the slashee that went to print in 1990. Is there anything you regret?

Everything that didn't deal directly with the romantic relationship was entirely cut or reduced to almost nothing. This meant losing many threads, large and small, that I'd carefully interwoven to set up the ongoing mystery, continuing characters and plot elements in the Quartet as a whole. Drastic cuts: Darcy McGill's part, and she stars in the next book; the Song Family and Fontana brothers; Van's background with her father and the Crystal Phoenix ghost tenant; Van's superstitious quirks.

I did regret "wasting" one element on the Quartet: it was written so that, with all the shady characters hanging around, readers wouldn't realize that this "Midnight Louie" narrator was the black cat they'd been seeing until the very last words, when Nostradamus makes it clear. But all the red herrings in this plotline were cut from the first edition of the book. I would have liked to use the same gimmick in the first Midnight Louie mystery, but couldn't, because I always saw the Quartet as the predecessor of the mystery series. I believed it would get in print again someday.

You started my mystery series in *Catnap* in 1992 with the murder of an editor in chapter one. Do I detect a personal interest?

I *have* threatened to write a "Dead Editor" series. Writers depend upon the competence and conscience of their editors, and, in some segments of publishing, writers can be exploited by substandard contracts as well as over-controlling editors. When an editor edits well, the author has no better friend. I should add that I've been an editor myself, both in journalism, and now in two anthologies of short stories, *Marilyn: Shades of Blonde* and *Midnight Louie's Pet Detectives*.

There you go, Madam Editor, taking undue credit! *I* edited *MLPD*. Okay, I always enjoy a good sob story. Tell me just how bad it was when my Quartet was in limbo between 1985–1990.

Awful. I'd quit my newspaper job to make fiction my livelihood just eighteen months before turning in your Quartet. My agent, an older woman, went in for heart surgery and went directly into a nursing home afterward, where all she could say was "Thank you for calling," so I was on my own. Except for you, of course, Louie. Not only were none of my phone calls or letters answered by the quartet's editor for almost two years, but half my money was withheld that long.

Luckily, my two "surprise" national bestselling fantasy

novels in the early '80s had me heading for the *New York Times* bestseller list, according to the publisher's sales force. Unluckily, the editor of *those* books became angry because he hadn't picked me to sell so well. He rejected the next fantasy book, using the excuse that I was "writing too many other books for other people," which referred to *your* series. So the Midnight Louie Quartet ended up threatening my career and livelihood on two fronts. Maybe black cats *are* unlucky!

No way! I came through in the end, did I not? It is a wonder you have iced only one editor in our books. So how did you survive the unjust turn of events? Is this why you sometimes call me your "muscle"?

I've found that if you don't give up, setbacks may actually turn out to be for the best, or to be survivable, at least. Yes, you're my "muscle." While we often downtrodden writers may get used to publishing reversals, this time I had an independent, feisty cat as a co-author. No way was Midnight Louie, P.I., going to get diced, sliced and consigned to the scrap heap. You cats are so proud of your nine lives and landing on your feet. We writers need to be as durable.

Now would be a good time to tell the folks about Midnight Louie, Inc., he said modestly.

Your one-cat comeback, you mean. When I do book tours, you are with me in spirit, if not body, because the Midnight Louie Adopt-a-Cat program brings homeless cats into bookstores during my autographing events. We find good homes for both felines and fiction, always a good cause. You now have your own webpage <http://www.catwriter.com/cdouglas>, which I struggle to update when not serving as your personal secretary. You have your own T-shirt; a twice-a-year newsletter, *Midnight Louie's Scratching Post-Intelligencer*; and a tip sheet on

Making Your New Cat Feel at Home. People wanting information on any of these can use your own address: PO Box 331555, Fort Worth TX 76163. You've done pretty well for a formerly homeless alley cat.

Well, I had a little help from my friends, and a lot more from my readers, Bastet bless 'em.